CELTIC
Storms

CELTIC STEEL {1}

AUTHOR OF HISTORICAL ROMANCE
AND SENSUAL FANTASY

DELANEY
RHODES

CELTIC *STORMS*

By DELANEY RHODES

Delaney@DelaneyRhodes.com
http://www.independentauthornetwork.com/delaney-rhodes.html

Celtic Storms

Celtic Steel Series, Book 1

Darina O'Malley watched the sun set in the bay from the great tower in O'Malley castle. She said a silent prayer for her cousin, Kyra, hoping the message that was delivered to the MacCahan's did not spell sudden doom for her and her people. If what her Uncle Ruarc had told her was true, she was to be married to a stranger in nearly a fort night, and her world would turn upside down.

The realization that her clan held secrets which could destroy them forever - chilled her blood. Who was this son of a Laird that she was betrothed to and how would he react when he learned the truth?

Celtic Storms

Copyright © 2012 by Delaney Rhodes

DR Publishing

ISBN: 9781470018924

Cover Design by Kim Killion

Edited by A. McConnell

Dedication

To my loving and infinitely patient husband – without you my life would be incomplete. To my daughters who have no idea how much they teach me.

ONE

MacCahan Castle - Northern Ireland - Fall 1457

"Patrick! Patrick!" repeated the annoying sound from the castle grounds. "Patrick!" The sound was getting closer as was the rhythmic tempo of approaching footsteps, as they navigated the muddy grounds. "Patrick - you are to be married", declared the voice sounding somewhat out of breath. "Your father has said it is so. "You," the boy bent over to catch his breath and hold his sides. "You must come at once, the Laird has requested you in his chambers," declared Braeden, matter-of-factly and quite loudly over the sound of rain. "And I am to accompany you to the O'Malley strong hold for fostering. Isn't that grand, Patrick? Isn't it?"

"Braeden, you know how Patrick despises an interruption while he works," stated Airard, the village black smith, quite sternly. "Whatever is this non-sense you speak of?" questioned Airard, who was more than remotely acquainted with eleven year old Braeden's vivid imaginings. In all of his sixty and two summers, Airard had never known a child so precocious, or so talented at story telling. Braeden had a knack for weaving tales and spinning webs that rivaled the most popular gossip. It would come as no surprise if Braeden became the village storyteller someday. *Yes, Braeden will make a fine bard one day, indeed.*

Twenty-six year old Patrick MacCahan never looked up from his work. Not even a glance. Sweat covered his brow and his concentration wavered as he continued to stoke the intense fire before him. As the eldest son of Laird MacCahan, Patrick had a reputation for patience that had undoubtedly come from his mother, Bevin.

"Patrick! The Laird must see you at once," stated Braeden. "There is much to be done to prepare for the journey to the O'Malley keep and not a second to waste according to your father. Come quickly lest you rouse his temper, Patrick."

Patrick had just heated the iron to the exact temperature he needed and was ready to begin forging the steel when he was interrupted. *For the love of the gods, what now?* It was the

7

second time within the week he had been interrupted by Braeden while working on the sword to be given to his youngest brother, Payton. *How is a man supposed to work with such noise? It would make him daft.*

"And you thought to escape the bounds of matrimony Patrick," laughed Airard. "It appears the bells toll for you this day Patrick," Airard quipped through clenched teeth.

"You and I both know you are mis-mis, you are no doubt mis-mistake- mistaken, Airard," stammered Patrick, throwing Airard a frigid glare. "Tis nothing more than a humorless j-je-je-jest."

"Ah, my friend, I wish it were so," replied Airard, his tone taking on a serious nature. Airard stood beside Patrick as he worked on the weapon and then placed a hand on his shoulder in condolence.

"T-te-te-tell me wh-wha-what you know." Patrick had never questioned that he would not marry. After all, what did he have to offer any lass? Sure, he was the Laird's eldest son, and he was well respected. But he stammered, and he had but partial use of his right hand. Even though he had trained intensely and become a fine black smith, it was hardly what the women of his village sought in a match. *I can't even speak to them. They*

8

avoid me. I frighten and confuse them, and I have not the countenance of my brothers.

Patrick stood head and shoulders above his brothers. By far the tallest man in his clan; he had an imposing size that garnered respect from men and awe from women. He was not as hard to look upon as he suspected, but he had not the form or face that made the lasses seek him out as they did Parkin, his younger brother, and middle son of Laird MacCahan. Parkin was never without female company, and tales of his prowess had spread throughout the neighboring clans, so much so that Laird MacCahan feared he would never make a match for Parkin, because his reputation preceded him.

With his imposing size, Patrick was a picture of a man. Long shoulder length chestnut hair laid in waves down his back and green eyes, the color of newborn leaves, graced his chiseled face. It was only when he tied his hair at the nape of his neck that one could really see him for the handsome man he was. Although Patrick wasn't aware, he had been the object of many a temptress in his village, but none had succeeded in securing his hand. He had more important things to do than waste his time on the frivolities of romantic entanglements.

Yet, Patrick was no innocent. Nay. He had had his fair share of female company when the need arose, thanks to his uncles and his father's fighting men. They seemed to know the exact location of every ale house and brothel within a day's ride. The ventures were pleasant enough but he always seemed to leave with regret at having disappointed his company with his refusal to talk. *They would simply throw me out if they knew. Of course they expect to converse, they are after all, female.*

"I know what you're thinking Patrick, and you're wrong my son," stated Airard. "You have more to offer a lady than you think, and there is no reason you cannot have the home and family most men seek. You are after all, a Laird's son, with all the status and comfort that affords."

"B-bu-bu-but my hand," replied Patrick. "I am use-use-useless." Patrick held up his right hand for inspection. While it looked normal, it had been crushed and broken many years before and he had never fully regained the use of it, although it was hard to tell from simple observation. It was the grip that had never fully come back. He would likely never wield a sword with his right hand again, at least not accurately. It was what caused him to begin using his left. His Uncles had ensured he was just as adept with his left as he had one day been with his right.

"Nay, I will not hear such nonsense from you," declared Airard. "You are a keen warrior and simply the finest black

10

smith in all of Northern Ireland, and you can wield a sword better than any of your brothers, even if it is with your left hand," replied Airard. "You can thank your Uncle Fionn for that."

It was true. Fionn had worked tirelessly to ensure that Patrick had a proper training in fighting. Even when his own father would no longer permit him to spar with the others, Fionn had taken him aside, and to neighboring villages to practice the art. Patrick was as good as any soldier out there, and even more daunting when his challengers found him to be left handed. He could switch sword hands in the blink of an eye and catch his combatants unaware. It was a startling revelation indeed.

"Patrick! Are you coming? Your father awaits you; impatiently at that," exclaimed Braeden. "Let's go, I'm eager to hear the details of our journey and gather my things." *As if you have many things, Braeden. What am I going to do with a pestering child on a trip such as this? It will be the death of me.*

Patrick didn't miss the knowing stares and crude comments thrown his way in jest from his brothers and his uncles as he walked through the castle doors and through the great hall. Even when he had stopped to wash the mud from his boots just outside the castle doors, he suspected the servant Jarvis had snickered at his expense. Everyone knew that Patrick did not wish to marry, and that he had no use for the ladies. Although none of the men understood why.

It was apparent the way the kitchen servants came alive and openly gawked at Patrick - that he intrigued them - this giant of a man with few words. A hushed and reverent silence fell over the keep whenever he entered to attend to clan business or to break his fast. If Patrick didn't know, or couldn't see the attention he received from the lasses, who was he to explain it to him?

Jarvis suspected it was a result of Patrick having grown up with little female interaction, and the many years of isolation and refusal to socialize that had turned Patrick into a hermit. "Nay, it is not my place to instruct the lad on matters of matching and loving," Jarvis murmured to himself, under his breath.

Payton wasted no time in aiming for Patrick. "Well, well dear *brathair*," his brother stated. "I hear you are betrothed?"

"Tis n-no-no-not so," stammered Patrick, "tis but a na-na-na-nasty rumor. One which I i-i-in-in-inten-intend to squash post haste." Patrick's face grew red as the emotion and embarrassment boiled in his blood.

How he hated being teased by his younger brothers when it came to the lasses. They made sport of it as often as possible, and their father had ensured that this time, they had plenty to go on. "Bo-both-bother me not, I have bu-bus-bus-business to attend to up-stairs."

Patrick managed to skirt past the entire great hall filled with those gathered for the noon meal without stopping, and reluctantly took the stairs that led to the third floor master's chamber three steps at a time. *I might as well get this over with. Father will be unhappy, but he will see things my way.*

The entire clan had come alive with wild speculation just three nights previous when the messenger arrived with an urgent missive from Laird O'Malley. It was even odd the way it was delivered. They had never had a missive from a clansman who remained seated on his steed at the Castle Gate.

Fionn was aghast that the messenger remained on his perch, taken aback by his lack of protocol, and therefore he deemed it necessary to request the messenger step down in order to size him up. But alas, the messenger stepped down as requested; only to mount the steed mere minutes afterwards when Laird MacCahan's reply was received, sending the messenger on his way once more.

Everyone had taken the missive to be a foretelling of the arrival of the three soldiers from the O'Malley clan who had arrived last eve, well past dusk. They were promptly gathered in Laird MacCahan's solar, and hadn't been seen since - yet most had figured that Jarvis had attended to them, and set them up with chambers on the servants' side of the fortress.

Even Braeden had managed to garner the names of the O'Malley clansman, as was customary, his queries unyielding until some reluctant maidservant had relented. They were Ruarc O'Connell, brother in law to Laird O'Malley and captain of the O'Malley soldiers; along with Deasum MacNaultey, Carbry O'Quinn, and Aengus O'Connell, another brother of the late Lady O'Malley.

What on earth do they want with the MacCahan's? They are one of the wealthiest clans in Ireland. Surely, they've no need for a Laird's son, thought Patrick as he winded the staircase.

"Father, I a-a-a-am here."

TWO

O'Malley Castle - West Coast, Ireland

Darina O'Malley paced back and forth in the great hall with such fervor that her best friend and younger sister, Dervila feared she would wear holes in the rugs that lay about the stone floor. "What troubles you Darina"? Dervila asked.

"What could Ruarc be thinking?" replied Darina. For as long as Darina could remember, she had trusted her uncle Ruarc - and he had never let her down - or mishandled her trust. But this new development, the one he refused to discuss with her before heading out with his men, had her puzzled.

It had only been three nights since their father Dallin O'Malley had succumbed to his heart issues. He had lived a long and noble life, and yet, the stress from his own wife's untimely death of the fever had taken its toll. He was seemingly in good health, having survived many battles and squirmishes over the years; but still his fifty-three summers had proven too much for him.

With no sons to speak of, Dallin had loved his 5 daughters like none other. Darina, his eldest, was seventeen summers, but in no way capable of leading a clan. Although he wasn't sure what choice there would be if the alliance with the MacCahans was not forged.

That's when he sought the counsel of his brother in law, Ruarc. Ruarc was a man of few words, but wise beyond his years, and known in the village as a fair and just leader. He had a close relationship with his sister's family and took great care with the O'Malley lasses from the day they were born, as if they were his own.

Dervila O'Malley was a bright and inquisitive girl of seventeen summers, who enjoyed working with the clan's scribe and map-maker. Just ten months younger than Darina, she was close to her sister in ways that could not be described.

Daenal, Darcy and Dareca O'Malley were always together; joined at the hip and busy managing the day to day affairs of the keep. Daenal had a keen interest and proven talent in the kitchens, while Darcy was familiar with dress making, having shipped much of her trade to export in her short fifteen summers. She was known far and wide as the best dress maker in Western Ireland, and in fact, some English noblemen had commissioned wardrobes for their ladies on more than one occasion.

Dareca, at only thirteen summers, showed promise as a weaver and the great hall was adorned with several of the most richly constructed tapestries in their region.

"I simply cannot believe that father has instructed Ruarc as he said," stated Darina. "Why wouldn't he have at least consulted with me? An arranged marriage to a MacCahan?" *There is no need. No need indeed.*

The O'Malley clan was one of the wealthiest of the Irish clans; a plethora of industry with their rich soil that combined with their sheep, pottery, stone and iron works made them wealthy beyond contemplation.

The O'Malley castle itself, sat upon a rock shelf above a cliff overlooking the bay. From the towers, the twin islands sat nearly one fall to the northwest of the village. For as long as she could remember, Darina had spent her evenings in the tower watching the sun set over the bay. Yes - the O'Malley lands were formidable. Situated between the Partry Mountains and the sea; the castle was a fortress nigh impenetrable by any foe.

The high castle rivaled that of Roman temples with its many domes, vaults and arches. The towers themselves were rounded

17

domes, rather than the traditional squared off boxes which were more common. Laird O'Malley had commissioned the plans from a Roman architect he had met in Edinburgh and it had taken near to four summers to complete construction. Although it maintained some of the standard Irish elements, it was profoundly unique. Nearly three dozen hired Norseman had aided in the construction, at a costly coin, but Laird O'Malley insisted it was necessary.

At fully five floors high at its peak, the high castle was an imposing site atop the cliffs and was surrounded on three sides by twelve foot high stone walls with archer stations positioned every thirty paces. The detail in the castle was intricate. Laird MacCahan had imported an untold amount of stained glass art which adorned the outer castle walls and entry ways. Most of the bed chambers contained actual glass windows as opposed to skins which covered the openings in the villager's huts.

The high castle was enormous. Quite possibly one of the largest three in all of Western Ireland and the O'Malley sisters each had their own bed chambers and attached ante-chamber sitting rooms. The O'Malley family proper and special guests were housed in the main part of the keep on the Western side overlooking the rocky cliffs and bay.

There were five floors in the Western wing. The top floor belonged to the Laird and contained the master's solar and bed chamber, meeting rooms and private banqueting halls. The servant's quarters were in the south tower; three full floors of them. The unmarried soldiers maintained quarters in the eastern wing, and the central portion of the castle was maintained as a common area for the clan's use - containing the great hall, the kitchens, the brewery and the storage housing.

Weapons were the O'Malley clan's chief industry and because their strong house was situated on the Western Coast, their exports had nearly quadrupled in the previous ten years; lending the O'Malley's to a formidable and wealthy status. There were four black smiths in the clan and they remained busy with commissions from merchants and neighboring clans.

"It's the curse, the damnable curse! I tell you, had it not been for the nonsense of the curse, Father would never have agreed to this", exclaimed Darina.

"You can't tell me you don't believe the curse is real, Darina, can you?" asked Dervila.

"Of course I can. It's nonsense; we have just had a streak of bad luck. There is no truth at all to the curse, and I cannot let some old wives tale rule the rest of my life. Now help me figure out how to get out of this!"

It had been twenty-two long years since a male child had been born to the O'Malley family. Twenty two years. Story had it that the Burke priestess had cursed Dallin O'Malley when he refused her to wife. No doubt she was a beautiful girl, but Dallin only had eyes for Anya. And Laird O'Malley wasn't about to force his son to marry Odetta Burke; even if it meant foregoing a major alliance with a neighboring clan. Odetta Burke had a reputation and none of it good.

Darina's grandsire had a deep appreciation for the affairs of the heart, having been joined in love for nigh to forty summers with his own wife. Darina's mother, Anya O'Connell, was the first born of the hired ship builder and was a peculiarly attractive girl, with bright green eyes and long auburn hair that fell down to her waist in tight ringlets; although she wore it braided and covered most of the time.

Anya was every bit the lady of the keep and well respected by the warriors as well as clans people. She had a knack for making well with others and many came to her to judge minor disputes and issues, leaving the major issues to the Laird.

It had been Anya's keen ability to manage the house hold and knack for turning industry into coin that had made the O'Malley clan into an impressive enterprise. Never had a woman been more loved than Anya O'Malley. Her untimely death had broken the heart and spirit of Laird O'Malley.

Anya's brother Rory's aptitude for boat and ship making had launched the clan into a profitable export industry that secured the future of the people for generations to come. He had joined his father in ship building practically since the time he could walk and oversaw the expansion of the piers and the port.

O'Malley castle's location on a bay port ensured their import and export trade business and brought merchants and buyers from all over the coast lines of Ireland. With their prime location, the clan's people had grown their enterprise and economy to near staggering size.

Rory's wife, Atilde, managed the clan's inn, which was situated along a path rising up from the piers just to the northeast of the furthest ship launch on the bay side. The three-story inn boasted sixteen chambers, a wash house, an ale house and stables for guests. There were also four small cottages that surrounded the inn that offered guest families more privacy. Many merchants who came for market days stayed over from time to time and there was always plenty of room and hospitality for others. Atilde saw to that.

The clan had their own chapel, attended by a local Priest, Father MacArtrey; although some of the clan still revered the pagan history of their ancestors. Theirs was a jolly mixture of mythical beliefs and pseudo-Catholic doctrine that suited them well.

Indeed - they had grown - my how they had grown. There was near to five hundred lives in all that resided within the bounds of O'Malley castle, many were servants, many were hired soldiers and the rest were family. The O'Malley clans people themselves had exceeded three thousand at last count, yet less than one hundred adult males remained. The youngest was nigh close to twenty-five summers and the eldest was Lucian.

Lucian was nearly seventy-three summers and suffered because of a stooped back from all his years serving as the clan *Sgriobhadair*. As the clan's scribe, Lucian had been responsible for keeping the clan genealogy records, death, marriage and birth records and making maps and charts for the ship captains. He had been more than happy to apprentice Dervila in his arts, having lost his own wife and daughter to the fever many years before.

22

Regardless that no male children had been born to the O'Malley clan for twenty two years; the clan survived, thrived and grew. There was no shortage of hands in the land, as the women had learned to perform all manner of duty and were treated as equals - and rightly so.

The look of surprise on the men's faces when merchant ships came to dock at port and were assisted by women was seldom hidden. But - it took no time for such details to become irrelevant as many of the merchants learned firsthand just how profitable their business would be in O'Malley land.

Now - the sight of women in men's apparel was another thing. It had taken some getting used to. In fact it had been Darina who championed the effort more than any other. It was simply impossible to work the docks and assist the merchants with unloading the goods and tying off the ships wearing women's clothes. Mishaps resulting in plunges into the bay were worsened by the fact that the women's attire was heavy and made it difficult to swim.

Dallin had given in to Darina several years prior, but had only agreed that women could wear tunics and truis that were clearly distinguishable from those worn by the men, either by color or texture. The truis was a type of trouser worn by the men that fit snuggly about the legs and tapered to just above

23

the calves. Often fashioned of leather, the women opted for opulent colors made from rich velvet. Worn with a long tunic which draped well past the knees, with long enveloping sleeves that fell just past the wrist; the O'Malley women had been the first in Ireland to fashion a suit of trousers just for women. Darcy had out done herself. Combined with a knotted leather belt and often draped with a tartan; the attire was functional and attractive.

Yes, Dallin O'Malley had agreed reluctantly - but only because it was practical. Even then he ordered that the women could only wear the attire while working; and that feasting, banqueting and attending to services at the chapel required proper dress as was befitting an O'Malley.

There was not a single task that an O'Malley female couldn't perform. In fact, some of the most avid hunters belonged to the O'Malley clan and often their tables were overflowing with the best venison and wild game that was available. There was also an abundance of fish and sea creatures with which to choose from and vegetables and fruit alike for which clans from all around would come to purchase on market day each week.

Except for the marked absence of youthful men in the O'Malley clan, one would hardly deem the strong hold as

24

deficient. Over the years, the elder men had managed to teach the women to protect themselves and had fashioned for them daggers, swords and bows befitting a woman; weapons that could either be easily hidden under their skirts or carried in baskets, such that no man could take them by surprise. Although, many wore them sheathed to their belts in plain sight; Darina had opted to fasten hers about her ankle just over her boots.

The O'Malley's were one of the first clans to train female soldiers, as was necessitated by the lack of strong young males. Dallin and Ruarc had also managed to gain the attention and loyalty of many warriors who worked for coin along the years and had put many to task. Most that came were young and virile but the vast majorities were already married and quickly brought their families with them.

After the high castle had been built, Dallin had seen to it that the former strong house become the quarters of the *bonnachts*. These commissioned soldiers, along with Ruarc, had taken up residence in the prior castle. Ruarc, and his family, occupied the wing which contained the master's quarters. Soldiers of station also occupied the former castle, while those of lower ranks dwelt in cottages interspersed throughout the village at strategic points.

Still, in spite of the integration of paid warriors into their clan, none of the families had yet to birth a male child. Even outsiders, it seemed, were destined to be affected by Odetta's curse; although Darina refused to believe it had anything to do with some mythical declaration spouted by a woman scorned who was devoid of her wits.

Odetta Burke had never married and remained on Burke lands situated just to the northeast of the O'Malley clan. There had been tales of her mystical powers and rumors abounded as to the validity of the curse. No one dared cross her for fear of her retribution, but Darina was not daunted in the least.

"Darina! Darina, are you listening to me?" Dervila repeated herself over and over until she thought she would lose her voice. It was only when she grabbed her sister roughly by the arm that Darina's haze broke.

"What did you say?" retorted Darina.

"I said - are you listening to me?"

No I'm not listening to you - you ninny. I haven't the time for this nonsense.

"I'm sorry, I must have been daydreaming. What did you say?" said Darina.

"Change has come, Darina. This is it — you must prepare yourself."

THREE

Central Ireland

Kyra O'Connell had been riding for nearly three days non-stop from MacCahan castle. She had barely paused since leaving the strong hold to slumber or eat for fear that time would run out. She had to get back to O'Malley lands, to her cousin Darina, to give her the news and instructions from her father Ruarc. No doubt, Darina would not be pleased. Laird O'Malley had been clear in his instructions to Ruarc and Kyra, just days before, knowing his time was coming to an end.

Although Ruarc was more than capable, Dallin had no intentions of making his brother-in-law the clan's new Laird. Ruarc had his hands full preparing the warriors, protecting the strong hold and overseeing the port and ship operations with Rory. There were new soldiers coming for coin and much preparation to be made with the building of the new ring fort to the north of the Castle to house the new soldiers and their families. There was no time for him to run the keep or maintain the enterprises and act as counselor and judge as well for the village's people. And - he was gaining in age.

Darina was the obvious choice as Laird, but being female, they would be hard pressed to find any adjacent clans who would respect her with the position. She had already gained much respect within her own clan. In fact, they had been coming to her for nearly two years to mediate minor disputes and settle matters between the villagers. She had taken much turmoil off of her father's back and she had learned well the skills to mediate controversies from her mother. Everyone seemed to respect her.

After all, Darina was blessed with the Laird's non-nonsense approach to decision making and her mother's unwavering fairness. Although her own clan would no doubt swear their loyalty to her - neighboring clans would not have a woman in such a place of power. No - a marriage was the most obvious way to form a strong alliance and placing a respected laird's son in the clan as her husband would accomplish everything Dallin had sought.

In fact, Dallin had made his decision nearly eleven years before and set it to writing with the assistance of Lucian the scribe. His decree was to be carried out and his instructions were sealed only to be opened on the day of his death. There was no explanation, no reasoning, and just a few simple words for

Ruarc's eyes only. Lucian has done his duty and Ruarc was informed about the sealed dictate on the day that Dallin passed.

There were no men of stature among the clan for Dallin's daughters to marry. As much as it pained him to think of sending his daughters to neighboring clans, he knew his only alternative was to bring men to O'Malley lands; that would be hard to do – if they knew the truth. With the opening of the dictate, Dallin had set in motion a series of events that would forever alter the lives of his family, his clan and his legacy.

When Ruarc called for Kyra to ride to the MacCahan fortress with an urgent message, he had been withholding and mysterious. Even the message itself made no sense to Kyra, but she took it nonetheless. It simply read, "It is time."

***

I was lucky – extremely lucky. By the goddess, I don't know what I would have done if they had seen me. Kyra knew what would have happened indeed. If any of the soldiers she had passed en route to MacCahan Castle had known she was a woman, she would most likely have been violated and killed.

As it was, her chain mail, cloak and helmet did much to protect her, but her shorn hair was her saving grace. It had pained her mother so to see her shear her hair to just above her shoulders, but her father understood. Her shoulder length copper hair was often matted and pressed flat against her face after wearing her helmet. Kyra managed to style it attractively when not riding, incorporating intricate braid work throughout the crown and adding flowers when available. She was no less beautiful because of it and all the merchants took notice.

Nay, if Kyra was to be safe, she would have to make sure she went undetected, and though her cloak did much to hide her womanly curves; long hair would make it near impossible to shade the truth. She was a soldier - and a good one. It had only been in the last ten months that her father had allowed her to act as messenger between clans; a task previously left for her older brother Kean. But since Kean's accident, he had been unable to ride for longer than a day at a time, and Kyra was so at ease on a steed, they had no other choice.

Her tall frame and wide shoulders gave her the daunting look of a fierce enemy when the situation called for it and no one had questioned her as she delivered and received messages between the clans.

Not even when she was asked to step from her horse, did any of the MacCahan sentries suspect she was anything but a fellow soldier. It was a blessing that warriors were men of few words. A curt nod or gesture could communicate volumes, and seldom was Kyra required to use her voice. *I've done well this time. Father will be most pleased. I just wish that Darina were as pleased to hear my news.* But she knew she wouldn't be – and she hated to be the one to tell her.

Her ride to MacCahan castle had been mostly uneventful; even the first day when she had to make her way through Burke territory. The Burke's were known for their morbid appetites for war making and pagan magic, but not for their strategy. It was almost easy to slip through the borders as long as one traveled at night; their soldiers never did well keeping watch after the sun had gone down.

Once, long ago, the Burkes and the O'Malley's had formed a strong alliance and treaty. When Dallin had refused Odetta's hand, the elder Burke became infuriated unleashing a storm of petty attacks against the O'Malley clan which only escalated after his death. When Odetta's brother, Cynbel took power, the petty attacks had turned into outright battles.

No longer were they dealing with the loss of a few dozen sheep or ruined crops. Nay – the Burke's had begun burning the cottages, kidnapping women and children and had even stolen several small merchant ships. They particularly liked stealing children for ransom and several had never been returned; although they always denied their involvement in the ransoms. Odetta had seen fit to send tokens of their esteem she called "gifts" to the O'Malley girls.

For as long as Kyra could remember, she and the O'Malley sisters had received periodic gifts from Odetta. No one really understood how they arrived, or who brought them - but they all knew who they were from. Yet someone was sneaking them onto O'Malley lands. Many had arrived on merchant ships, or been placed on the docks with the rest of the deliveries only to be brought to the rightful sister on the daily routes.

At first it appeared they were only dark jokes of some kind. A beautiful roll of tapestry or material when laid out would contain a large blood stain, or sheep hoof, a box of broken trinkets, a dead rabbit in an intricate gold box. But when Dervilla opened a small jewel chest which housed the pinky finger of a small child - Dallin knew that things were deeply serious.

It was then that Dallin and Ruarc determined that the women had to be trained to protect themselves and defend their families. The soldiers had begun making rounds throughout the

33

village each night to ensure that everyone had arrived home safely and was where they should be.

A curfew was instituted so that anyone unaccounted for by nightfall would be assumed missing and a group of soldiers would be sent to search. Even banquets and celebrations were to be cut short so that everyone could retire prior to night fall.

Nothing had raised the ire of Ruarc O'Connell more than the realization that for months his daughter, Kyra, and niece Darina had been sending messages of their own to Odetta. Darina had made arrangements to have a merchant drop messages and packages at the Burke castle on his way through Burke lands with his wares. The last message they managed to send had been simple. A Burke plaid which had been wrapped around a pile of sheep dung lay on a bed of velvet in a turquoise encrusted chest.

They had bribed the textile merchant to obtain the Burke plaid and paid dearly for it, but it communicated exactly what Darina thought of Odetta's nonsense. It wasn't until after Odetta tortured and imprisoned the merchant that they had been unable to continue the ruse.

Ruarc had made it abundantly clear to then fifteen year old Darina that he was displeased and had punished Kyra by refusing her to ride or assist in the stables for an entire harvest. He had not told Dallin though - and for that - the girls were grateful.

Ruarc knew that Darina had no patience for Odetta, and that she believed the stories of magic, mayhem and curses were nonsense. Darina had hoped that Odetta would cease her inept attempts at intimidating her, but Odetta never did. It seemed it mattered not whether Darina took her seriously - the villagers did, her parents did and Ruarc did. And Darina's life would never be the same because of the wretched woman. She would forever be a prisoner in her own village.

Somehow, Odetta still seemed to have her spy amongst the O'Malley's. Darina had continued to receive messages from Odetta every fortnight for near to two summers. They had become more brazen of course, with Odetta clearly identifying herself in the letters. The direct messages were polite, enigmatic and almost poetic. If one hadn't known better, one would have assumed them to be friends.

Oh - there was always an underlying threat to Odetta's missives; one that Darina needed no help in deciphering. When Ruarc finally gave up his quest to intercept every package delivered to the keep, Darina was able to oblige Odetta's request to converse.

FOUR

MacCahan Fortress

Patrick hesitated as he alerted his arrival in the master's chambers. No doubt his father would have much to say, and Patrick, as usual, would struggle to speak his mind. It was not a new dilemma, and Patrick was certainly not the only one who had dealt with it. His mother, brothers and even the Laird's fighting men knew all too well the power of Laird MacMahan's intellect and sharp tongue. It was never wise to question Laird MacCahan. *But I must try.*

Not only was Breacan MacCahan a well-spoken and educated man; he was a force to be reckoned with. He seldom held his tongue long enough for anyone to break his narrative. Getting a word in on any dialogue was a challenge. Most people simply waited until he had finished his dissertation before daring to interject any banter of their own.

Patrick had heard talk of an impending alliance with another clan but not in any of his twenty-six years had he suspected any such alliance would involve a marriage rite. Although it was still accepted to form allegiances through marriage, it was not at all customary for the MacCahan's. It had been over two hundred years since an arranged marriage had occurred among any of the MacCahan clan, and even then the bride and groom had known each other and grown up in neighboring villages.

This cannot be. Why would my father ever agree to marry me off to some poor girl who has never even met me? She won't even have the opportunity to reject me. Besides I am well passed marrying age. Rosmerta's tit! How did this happen?

Patrick stumbled over a large clump of rock and earth which stuck immovable in the middle of his path along the road back up to the castle. He was covered in mud and drenched through but sensed a stop to bathe would garner his Father's wrath. It had rained - nay - it had stormed for nearly five fort nights making the ground and everything around it a muddy mess of tangled earth and waste. It was near impossible to traverse the broken ground in any haste and no doubt his father would be growing impatient the longer it took him to arrive.

How much more rain can there possibly be? If it doesn't stop soon, we are in danger of losing more cottages and the crops will be all but worthless. The flooding will only worsen and it will be nigh impossible to travel as most of the roads are nearly impassable. Perhaps I shall have a reprieve from travel until the storms desist?

The MacCahan clan had lost five cottages to the incessant storms; several livestock, a large portion of the western castle wall and many lives. The storms had come upon them so quickly they were ill prepared to cope. When it became obvious that there was no sign of letting up, Laird MacCahan had opened the doors to the great fortress to all of the outlying villagers, setting the men up in the great hall and the women and children in the servants quarters.

The MacCahan castle sat high upon a hill overlooking the lands and streams. It had been nearly three fort nights since the villagers came to stay and still it continued to rain. When the stream overflowed and carried livestock and villagers alike towards the sea, Patrick and his brothers had rushed to rescue those they could. As it stood, they had lost some farmers, the clan baker and the black smith's youngest grandson.

When Patrick's step mother made an attempt to save a child lodged on the roof of one of the cottages, Monae had lost her footing and fell through the roof, causing the structure to collapse. Monae had been swept out to sea with the others. Their bodies were never found and Breacan MacCahan had mourned the death of his wife in solitude and silence. Breacon MacCahan had mourned the loss of two wives, and the toll was obvious in his face.

Patrick's mother had been killed when he was but 12 years old. Before his very eyes, he watched as the mercenary sliced his mother's side clean through to her rib cage. Just three years younger, nine year old Parkin had begun to scream and wail at the sight of the man from behind the trees. Despite Patrick's efforts to keep him quiet; Patrick knew he must do something. Finally, Patrick could do nothing else but bind Parkin's mouth with his plaid in hopes he wouldn't be heard.

They had all gone to the stream to fish and bathe as was customary with their mother on warm summer days. Patrick and Parkin had taken up the lead, running ahead of the others. Younger brother Payton, only seven summers old, was languishing behind as was usual and had yet to arrive at the stream. The look of sudden horror on his mother's face gave away that they were in imminent danger.

As his mother turned towards the village, Patrick saw him. An angry brute of a man with long unkempt hair, wearing sparse chain mail that appeared to be several years older than he, and sitting atop the largest horse he had ever seen. Blonde almost colorless hair that hung past his shoulders and crystal blue eyes, spoke the truth. This man was a Norseman.

Patrick panicked for a moment, awe struck at the massive brute in front of him and simultaneously impressed with his mother's fortitude. From behind the patch of trees, he and Parkin hid and watched. *I must help her. She is but a woman and I am trained in defense. What can I do?*

"Who are you", questioned Bevin MacCahan, Patrick's mother. "And what are you about?" The tilted smirk that the Norseman revealed told Patrick everything he needed to know, and it was not good. The imposing figure strode closer to Bevin. "I will have your jewels my lady - and your brooch." She had worn the MacCahan clan brooch with her plaid that morning, and it was indeed spectacular with its exquisite detail and inlaid sapphire and ruby stones.

"Nay" stated Bevin, almost nonchalantly, "They are not yours for the taking. They belong to Laird MacCahan, the chieftain upon whose lands you transgress."

"I will have them," answered the Norseman, "or else I will have your head."

Fear began to rise in Patrick, such that he thought he would lose his noon meal all over the ground where he stood with his brother.

"Nay! You will not touch a hair on her head, and you must leave at once," shouted Patrick as he came around the trees to stand ten paces from the Norseman. His hands shook so much - he hoped the warrior did not see. *What am I doing? What am I going to do? I cannot let him touch my family; Father will scorch me if anything should happen.*

"And who is this, may I ask?" inquired the daunting warrior. "'Tis no one", replied Bevin, "'tis but a simple stable boy who has wandered too far from the grounds - he is of no consequence and should return immediately to the keep," Bevin said as she gave Patrick a knowing glance and titled her head toward the castle grounds.

"Nay," said the Norseman, "I perceive he is more than a stable boy, and may bring a ripe handsome reward should he be the Laird's son - as is my suspicion."

"Mother, no," exclaimed Patrick, surprised at the untruth she had told. Patrick's heart stuck in his chest at the

magnitude of his utterance. In that one fleeting moment,
Patrick knew his life was about to change; drastically, and not
for the better.

"I will have them now," demanded the Norseman. "Nay," said
Bevin.

"I have told you they belong to Laird MacCahan, and they
will never be yours."

"You will hand them over now."

"Over my dead body," exclaimed Bevin as she unsheathed her
dagger from under her skirts.

"So be it," replied the man.

To this day, Patrick could not quite remember the exact
turn of events that resulted in his mother's death and his own
injuries. His mother's head lay still on the ground just two
feet from her body and Patrick's right hand was crushed and
broken, his mother's dagger in his left hand, bloodied from the
flesh of the Norseman's horse. Her brooch and jewels were gone,
taken by the trespasser.

It had taken several minutes for his father and captain of
his guards to arrive. His youngest brother, Payton had seen to
that. As soon as he spotted the stranger near the stream, he had

turned tail and ran towards the fortress. No doubt the Norseman had been scared off at the ferocious sound of a roar bellowed by Breacan MacCahan at the news of the intruder.

Parkin remained tied to the tree - where Patrick had left him; his plaid still bound about his mouth. Whimpering and struggling to breathe, Parkin's face and chest were drenched with tears for his mother and brother, and the regret of being unable to help.

Patrick's hand had healed well enough. He was still able to use it - the healer saw to that - but he would never have full use of it - and it would never be as strong as it once was. For a lad of just twelve summers, it was devastating news, especially for one destined to be the clan leader. As the eldest son, it was expected that he be the strongest, most skilled warrior, and that he have full use of all of his faculties - so as to protect his people.

It was the other that had changed Patrick's life forever. For nearly three summers afterwards - he had not spoken a single word. He had not climbed out of his haze, and not ventured a care for companionship. Three full summers - and still nothing.

The healer had all but given up hope that Patrick was still there, inside - somewhere. But Maeri was not akin to giving up.

43

The healer had seen men through worse. Men — yes, children — no. Most grown men could not withstand the sight of a beloved being struck down so viciously without succumbing to the darkness or drink. But Patrick was just a wee lad. To have witnessed such an atrocity was unspeakable. Indeed, it had rendered Patrick utterly speechless.

FIVE

Laird MacCahan's Chambers

"Patrick, my son, you are here. Please sit - we have much to discuss," stated the elder MacCahan. Breacan MacCahan was a handsome man, with long brown waves that flowed past his shoulders and tiny braids that sprung from his temples. He wore a full beard that touched near to the top of his breast bone and had blue eyes the color of rain.

"Thank you. I pr-pre-pre-prefer to stand," Patrick retorted.

"Nonsense, take a bench Patrick," commanded the Laird.

"Patrick, please welcome our guests from the O'Malley lands. Patrick, this is Ruarc O'Connell, he is the older brother of Laird O'Malley's wife and chieftain of the O'Malley military forces. His brother-in-law, the Laird, passed recently." Breacan gestured towards a stout looking red headed man dressed in soldier's attire who stood leaning against the south wall. Ruarc nodded his response.

"And this is Deasum MacNaultey his second in command, along with Carbry O'Quinn - his armory overseer and this is Aengus O'Connell, younger brother to the late Anya O'Malley - the Laird's wife." Patrick nodded his acknowledgement and his condolences.

"Patrick - they have come for our help," stated Laird MacCahan, matter-of-factly.

"Our help? I have heard tell of the O'Malley strong hold and I dou-dou-doubt they n-n-nee-need our help," Patrick retorted.

"Patrick!" Laird MacCahan roared. "You will hold your tongue," he urged.

"Nay," retorted Ruarc. "Tis an astute observation" he said as he walked towards Patrick and placed a fatherly hand on his shoulder. "Your son has the right of it, Breacan; he proves his intellect through his suspicion. I would expect nothing less." Ruarc bent down to sit, inviting Patrick to join him with a nod.

"Patrick, there is much that has been kept from you. And I mean to set it to rights."

46

"Ruarc," queried Breacan with a quizzical look, "What are you about?"

"'Tis only proper the lad be fully aware of what awaits him," replied Ruarc.

"Enough!" roared Patrick as he rose slamming his left fist down on the top of his father's table. "You sp-spe-speak as if I am not here; what is s-s-s-so important that I need be int-int-interrupted from my work?" asked Patrick.

"Let's have some ale, shall we?" interjected Aengus as he passed a mug to Patrick. "This will help."

***

Kyra was more than reluctant to return to O'Malley castle, for she knew she would be inundated with questions by Darina. *How do you explain to your cousin that her life is about to change, and she has no say over it? How do you answer the questions that you have no answers to?*

Kyra stepped from her horse and handed him over to Moya, the stablewoman. Moya had kept the clans horses for as long as Kyra could remember and there was none better to tend to them. Moya had a special touch that the animals seemed to understand

and respect. Not only were they extremely well cared for, Moya had seen to it that they were properly trained and could traverse even the most difficult terrain.

Moya had even taken it upon herself to outfit the clan with wagons and carpentoms which were two wheeled contraptions pulled by two horses - similar to Roman chariots. Very few clans in Ireland had such modern conveniences.

It was well past sundown, and Kyra was in dire need of a meal and a bath. She had been gone nearly seven nights. Although she knew that Darina would no doubt still be awake and eager with anticipation; she secretly hoped Darina would not wish to speak with her until the morn, so she could recuperate from her journey. But it would not be so.

Darina was anxious with anticipation. The past weeks had been long and arduous with first the death of her mother, then her father, and the sudden activities with her Uncle Ruarc leaving to MacCahan lands.

She vaguely remembered the conversation she had with her Uncle just before he sent Kyra to deliver a message - all the way to MacCahan castle. It had come upon the cloud of death in the castle. First, her mother had passed, then her father. Her sister's had become so grief stricken that they could barely function. After her sisters had taken to their beds, Darina had to send over to the islands for servants to maintain the keep.

It was not a quick jaunt to MacCahan lands. Nay - it was nearly a five day ride for an ordinary horseman. And Ruarc and his men had left the very next morning after Kyra's departure. "To prepare the way," Ruarc had said. "To ensure the agreement still stands and to secure the future of the O'Malley clan."

There was something in there about a betrothal and a marriage. I am to be married to a MacCahan? Lord how she wished she had had more time with Ruarc prior to his departure. *But, would it really have mattered?* Darina had been so busy seeing to her grieving sisters and preparing the services and burial rites for her parents, that she had scarcely the time to grieve herself.

She knew, as the eldest, what was expected of her, and she had done her best. The guilt at having not shed one tear nearly overwhelmed her and in its place an anger arose that matched nothing she had ever felt before.

Father MacArtrey had recognized it early on and sought out Darina so fervently she feared she would go daft. "I have nothing to speak with you about, Father", she reiterated. "I am perfectly fine. Let me be about my business."

"Ah - but I fear you are wrong my dear. There is much anger in you. With unharnessed anger comes much danger, Darina. Many things have happened in the last fortnight and you need guidance and counsel. Your clan needs you, and your anger threatens us all," he said.

But Darina had continued walking; passed the chapel towards the port to check on the day's deliveries. *Work will keep my mind off of the future. My life is no longer my own, and I have no choice in which direction to take. This cannot be what my father had wished for...*

SIX

MacCahan Castle

Eleven year old Braeden MacTierney had fostered with the MacCahan clan nigh since his birth. Laird MacCahan had gathered his boys the day after Braeden's arrival to explain that the babe's parents had perished in a ship wreck. Braeden had been brought to the clan for care by a priest from a neighboring village. Braeden's only remaining family was a pair of widowed noblemen who had not the fortitude to raise a wee *bairn*. They would, of course, see to the babe's comfort by providing coin and counsel, but the child needed to be reared in a community where he could learn and grown. They had even seen to it to provide the services of a wet nurse until the child could be weaned.

Patrick was fifteen summers the day that Braeden came to live with the MacCahans. Just three years after his mother's death. Patrick had barely spoken at all until the week that Braeden arrived. He took to the infant immediately, as if he sensed a loss and longing that were kindred between the two.

After all, the child had lost his parents and he had no voice of his own. Monae, Laird MacCahan's new wife, had taken the child to rear as one of her own. Having never had children herself, Monae gave unselfishly to the rearing of the child – and he made her proud.

Braeden was a precious child – loving, sweet and curious. He learned quickly and easily and sought to please everyone. Patrick was the perfect older brother to all his brothers, but Braeden especially had a fondness for Patrick that few understood.

Patrick regained much of the use of his voice just as Braeden was learning to speak. Although Braeden could be annoying, Patrick had an unyielding patience about him that others envied.

He had never anticipated leaving MacCahan castle. It had never entered his mind. He was to be the Laird of the MacCahan clan when his father wasn't able. As the eldest son, it was the way. Under no circumstances could Patrick envision a suitable reason that his father would change course so drastically and dramatically - and a forced marriage at that.

What have I done to displease my father so that he would put me out of my own clan? Are we in such need of a dowry that I am to be sold off as a hired hand?

The dowry would come in handy, that much was true. After all the turmoil the MacCahan's had suffered recently with the flooding, the loss of the crops and livestock, and the cost of rebuilding of the lost cottages - the coin would be welcome. *No - that couldn't be it.*

My father is a steadfast and reasonable man; no doubt we have plenty of stores to get us through the coming winter and long into the summer. Surely there is enough.

Patrick set the mug of ale down on the bench between him and Ruarc. He had only been in his father's chambers for a few moments, but already had a sense of foreboding he knew he could not shake. "What are you keeping from me father?" he questioned.

"Patrick, it has never been my intention to keep you in the dark about what has transpired. I only told you, and the rest of our clan what you needed to know to keep you safe," stated the Laird.

"I am a gro-grown man, Father!" retorted Patrick. "Ye've no need to hide matters from me. I've never once given ye any reason to believe I have a l-l-loo-loo-loose tongue!"

"Silence!" roared Breacan. "Hold your tongue Patrick so that we may speak."

Ruarc interjected, "Patrick - we have a very delicate matter for ye to attend to; one that is pivotal for the survival of my clan; one we will trust only to you. It is your rightful place and an honor and we have the utmost faith that you can carry out your destiny."

Ruarc reached over and placed a firm squeeze on Patrick's shoulder. He gripped his forearms and looked him right in the eyes. "Patrick - You are to be the new Laird of the O'Malley clan," he hesitated.

"And you are to return Braeden, unharmed, to his rightful home."

Patrick jumped at the words - startled at their meaning. *His rightful home? His parents are dead! He belongs with the O'Malleys?*

Ruarc sputtered and paced the length of Laird MacCahan's meeting room. He tugged at his long beard in introspection as if searching for the right words and how to cushion the blow. The other men nodded in support.

Ruarc spoke slowly and deliberately, "Patrick, when Braeden came to MacCahan castle, his parents were not dead. His parents were actually protecting him. There were certain individuals who wished to see the babe dead. So - Laird O'Malley chose to have Braeden brought here. You see Patrick - Monae was a distant cousin of Laird O'Malley's wife. Dallin O'Malley knew that he would be fostered well here and hidden amongst family."

"Patrick - Braeden is an O'Malley," interrupted Laird MacCahan. He continued, "Of course we took the child Patrick, we had no choice. Monae would not see the child in danger; we raised him as our own."

Aengus chimed in, "Patrick - Braeden is the only son of Dallin O'Malley."

Patrick's tongue caught in his throat. "I, I, don-don-don't know what to say."

"It is time Patrick," Breacan repeated after rising from his seat. "Braeden must be returned to his clan - to his people - to his sisters. With the death of Dallin, a new laird must lead the clan."

"B-b-but Braeden is too young."

"That is why we need you, Patrick," said Ruarc. "We need you as our new Laird. You are to marry the eldest O'Malley daughter, Darina, and continue to foster Braeden in O'Malley lands. Braeden is closest to you and he trusts you. You are the eldest MacCahan son - it is only fitting that you be Laird."

Patrick stood and surveyed the room - almost dizzy at the revelation of Braeden's identity. *How could they have kept this from me, and why in the world would it be necessary? The O'Malley clan is wealthy and well situated, what could cause them such fear that they would send their only male heir away to be raised by strangers?*

"Does Braeden kno-kno-know?" Patrick directed to Ruarc. "Nay - and we'd like to keep it that way for several more years, if possible. Patrick, his own mother did not know he survived the birth. Laird O'Malley insisted on that to make sure she would not reveal his whereabouts in an attempt to see him."

The registry says she birthed a female child that died shortly after delivery. And - Laird O'Malley never saw him again after he was born. He just made sure he was cared for here, and sent funds for his comfort," said Ruarc.

"So no one in the clan is aware of Braeden's existence?" asked Patrick.

"That's right Patrick, not even his five older sisters. You are to marry the eldest, Darina, in a fort night," stated Ruarc.

"Why the hurry Ruarc?" retorted Patrick. "That gives me naught sufficient time to make her acquaintance."

Deasum interrupted, "Patrick, as you know, the O'Malley lands are situated between the Partry Mountains and the sea. Ours is a growing shipping empire and market center in need of a leader. To the north of us lies the Burke territory. The Burke's have been at war with the O'Malley's for some time; this dispute threatens more than just the shipping concerns. The Burke's have taken to treachery, kidnapping and even murder in the past. We have no faith they will quell their efforts after learning of our Laird's demise."

Aengus chimed in, "It is the Burke's, Patrick, that we hide Braeden from, they would seek his death if they knew he were alive."

"Ruarc, were there no suitable men to be had in O'Malley territory?" questioned Patrick. "Nay Patrick," responded Ruarc. "None of your caliber; not a Laird's son or nobleman's son, and certainly no one more qualified to continue Braeden's rearing."

"I see," replied Patrick. "And what does this alliance do for the MacCahan clan?"

"Patrick!" shouted Breacan MacCahan.

"Nay, nay," responded Ruarc interrupting the Laird. "'Tis a reasonable question."

"Patrick we will see to it that the lost cottages are rebuilt, that your livestock is multiplied and that your father, the Laird will receive Darina's sizable dowry. We will also provide your clan with a shipping vessel, the likes of which you have never seen, and a suitable pier with launches, of course – we wish to do commerce with you. Soon, MacCahan lands will be known as a robust commerce port and you will have much enterprise," Ruarc continued gesturing toward Breacan.

Breacan interrupted, "Patrick we are strategically located on the coast and Ruarc has thought to launch a commercial port, here on MacCahan lands. It will be a prosperous undertaking, for both our clans."

"What of my brothers, and my father? Who will stand in my father's stead when he is no longer Laird?"

"Patrick, I have already spoken with my men, that won't be necessary for quite a while and Parkin will make a fine replacement", stated Breacan.

"And this is what you wish father?" inquired Patrick.

"It is," was his short reply.

"So be it then."

Patrick rose and walked out the door and down the hallway towards his chamber.

SEVEN

MacCahan Fortress

Patrick returned to his chambers, deep in reflection at all that had transpired and what was to come. He examined his chambers but could not imagine living anywhere else. The large hearth bared the remnants of a dissipating fire and shadows crossed the wall from the small window to the east of the hearth.

There was a six board chest at the foot of his bed and tapestries adorned his walls. A table sat to the right of the hearth, with two chairs. Another six board chest which had been fashioned with taller legs sat next to his bed. On either side of his bed and against the wall - hung weapons and armor that had been passed down from his grandsire.

It was nearing sun down and Patrick was growing weary. It was nearly time to dine in the great hall and he wasn't so sure he wanted the company. No doubt his brothers would show him no mercy in their taunting. *Perhaps I should send to the kitchens for my meal.*

A faint sound rustled on his bed, and he was suddenly aware that he was not alone. *Braeden. What on earth?*

The unmistakable sound of light snoring caused Patrick to chuckle. It wasn't the first time he had found Braeden in his bed, and it probably wouldn't be the last. Braeden had developed a fondness for Patrick early on. Since the first time that Braeden had jumped into his bed after Patrick had awakened; startled with a night terror.

Most in the MacCahan keep had grown accustomed to Patrick's night terrors. It was not uncommon to hear the blood curdling screams or crashes in the middle of the night from Patrick's chamber. They had begun after the death of Patrick's mother. The healer had tried all kinds of potions and elixirs to relax Patrick's mind so that he could rest instead of fitfully tossing about all evening. But none of them had worked.

For a while, his brothers and even Airard had taken their turn keeping watch at night over Patrick so they could wake him when the terrors came upon him. Eventually though, Patrick had managed to run his caregivers off. Their pity was in no way appreciated and he made that clear.

That's when Laird MacCahan had decided to move Patrick's room to the furthest chamber on the eastern wing of the keep near the servant's quarters. It had been where his grandsire had retired after the death of his wife, and Patrick felt instantly at home.

It hadn't taken long however for Braeden to locate Patrick. Even as just a toddler, Braeden's curiosity ruled his temperament. It was he on the first night that Patrick had spent in his new chambers that he came barreling through the door at Patrick's bellows.

"Paaaaa-tty, Paaaa-ttick," Braeden had called as he jumped into bed right beside Patrick. He wrapped his chubby toddler arms about Patrick's neck, and wiped his forehead with his night shirt.

"Braeden MacTierney, what on earth do you think you are doing?" called Mavis, Braeden's nurse. "Paaaa-ttick", answered Braeden, pointing to Patrick who lay next to him. "Come along with me now Braeden, we must get you back to your bed," replied Mavis. "Nay, nay," screamed Braeden who proceeded to throw a thorough screaming fit.

"You will wake the entire keep Braeden, come now and leave Patrick alone, he needs his rest," she said peering solemnly at Patrick through the candlelight. "Pease, oh pease, pease", Braeden begged in his high pitched toddler voice.

"Patrick, do you wish me to take Braeden with me?" asked Mavis. Patrick shook his head as he wrapped his arms around Braeden and they drifted off to sleep together. Braeden had shared Patrick's bed on many occasions since that first night. Braeden had a way of calming Patrick like none other.

The night terrors had lessened throughout the years and as Patrick grew, the grip the trauma had on him dissuaded. Airard and Braeden had become his closest companions. He gradually climbed out of his shell and regained his speech. Although he still stammered and sputtered, he was able to communicate what he wished - that is, when he wished it. There were few things that caused Patrick to seek conversation, but when he did, people tended to listen.

Wise beyond your years. That's what Airard had said. *A keen mind and a noble soul.* Patrick could only hope it was so. Growing up the eldest son of the Laird, with a broken fighting hand, a halting tongue didn't prove great promise.

Patrick bent down to wipe the hair from Braeden's face as he slept. In an instant, Patrick's world had turned upside down. He was to be married, and essentially he would be responsible for the remainder of Braeden's rearing. At some point in the future, he knew he would have to explain to Braeden about his parents, his sisters, and that his life was in danger.

The sound of thunder alerted Patrick to the lateness of the hour. No doubt Airard would wonder what had become of him and what had happened. Airard had been his mentor, his instructor and his closest friend. It would be hard to leave Airard behind and he would miss him greatly.

***

Patrick gently closed the door to his chamber, headed down the long corridor towards the stairways to the bottom floor and traipsed towards the kitchens. Glenia the castle cook was busy with setting out the meal. Several women worked feverishly loading platters and filling the mugs to be placed in the great hall. It was nearly time for the evening feast but Patrick knew he would spend his meal with Airard at his cottage.

He poked his head around the large stone hearth and gestured towards Glenia. "Pl-ple-please see that Braeden has his m-me-meal in my chambers, Glenia," Patrick requested.

"And what of yours?" inquired Glenia as she wiped a trickle of sweat which beaded on her forehead.

"I shall be with Air-Airard," he turned and exited the kitchens towards the back of the keep and headed towards the castle walls.

Patrick dreaded heading outdoors, but needed desperately to speak with Airard. Airard resided in a small cottage towards the back of the castle wall not far from the blacksmith's forge. There was a winding pebble path that led just past the stables towards the forge which sat on a slight hill and faced towards Airard's cottage.

Lightening broke across the sky lighting the path towards the cottage. A driving rain began just as he stepped outside the doors of the keep. *But of course it would rain now that I've seen fit to venture out.*

The smell of horse dung and mud hung in the air as Patrick fumbled towards the cottage with his cloak covering his head. He had grown accustomed to the rain and had gone through an abundance of clothing and linens in a short time. The wash women could barely keep up with their duties as it had not stopped raining and there was hardly anywhere to lay aside the freshly washed items to dry.

They had taken to hanging clothing and linens everywhere there was a spare spot near a hearth that could be found. It had irritated Airard so to see bed linens and table dressings hung near the hearth in his forge that Patrick feared he would succumb to the heart sickness.

I don't think I've laughed so hard in my life, Patrick thought to himself. If Patrick hadn't intervened, near half of the keep's bed linens would have ended up in the fire at the blacksmith's hut, but he was finally able to reason with Airard. Since the villagers had come to stay in the castle and littered the floors of the great hall each night; there was practically nowhere else for the linens to dry.

Thankfully Adreana had offered to see to meals for Airard each night in exchange for use of the hearth. Adreana was the eldest servant still working for the Laird and had been widowed almost fourteen summers. Her daughters had left MacCahan lands many seasons before after marrying into neighboring clans.

Adreana had maintained a keen interest in Airard for some time and taken this as her opportunity to showcase her skills in the kitchens. Airard was fond of her company and appreciated the meals, and especially of not having to spend his evenings alone. Patrick had teased him relentlessly since the uproar in the forge but Airard seemed not to care.

"Airard," bellowed Patrick as he wrapped his fist against the side of Airard's cottage. "Airard," he shouted again. *I certainly hope he can hear me over this rain.*

Patrick pushed the door a crack and peaked inside, the smell of roast duckling rose to meet him. Out of the corner of his eye he spotted Airard at the table breaking bread and filling Adreana's mug.

"Patrick, do come in my son," he said as he rose to greet him. "Let me take your cloak." Airard helped Patrick remove his dripping cloak and Adreana hung it on a peg near the hearth so that it would dry. "Won't you join us?" asked Airard motioning to the table.

"I do no wi-wi-wish to intrude Airard," replied Patrick. "Nonsense," stated Adreana. "Let me fetch you some food." Patrick gave Airard a knowing grin as Airard blushed and waved him off.

"I cannot believe it continues to storm," Airard stated loudly attempting to take Patrick's mind off his teasing. The sound of the fire splitting and food being dished briefly disguised the incessant patter of rain hitting the roof. In the corner near Airard's straw bed, Patrick could see a pail which caught the rain slipping through a crack in the thatched roof.

"I will see to the r-re-repairs tomorrow," stated Patrick, matter-of-factly. "Nonsense," retorted Airard, "you have more pressing matters to attend to."

Adreana returned to the table with a metal trencher piled high with vegetables and roast duck. "It smells wo-wond-wonderful," said Patrick giving her an appreciative nod.

"I must be off now Airard," Adreana stated. "But I will return tomorrow evening with your meal and I will be back at the forge in the morn to gather the linens."

"You shouldn't venture out in this rain alone my lady," said Airard. "Why don't you let Patrick attend you to the keep?"

"Nonsense," replied Adreana. "Besides, I am meeting Conri at the stables to assist with the new foal. He will see to my safe return."

Patrick and Airard sat in silence for several minutes after Adreana had left. They had finished their meal and cleared their dinner before reclining beside the fire. "Patrick, tell me what your father said."

"The sh-shor-short of it is that I am to be married in nearly a fort night. I am to take Bra-Brae-Braeden with me to O'Malley lands. I am betrothed to the deceased Laird O'Malley's el-el-eldest daughter, Dar-Dari-Darina - I think it was."

"O'Malley lands. I have heard tale of them. They are one of the wealthiest of clans, Patrick," stated Airard.

"Aye," replied Patrick. "'Tis so."

"I see," stated Airard. "And what of Braeden?"

"I am to con-cont-continue his fostering at O'Malley castle," stated Patrick as he picked the mud from his boots.

"And - you are alright with this?" queried Airard.

"Aye," said Patrick. "I am very fond of hi-him."

"Well then, what of this marriage?" questioned Airard with a raised brows.

"I haven't any s-s-say in the matter," retorted Patrick.

"But of course you do Patrick. Laird MacCahan is a just and reasonable man. I'm certain he would not force you if you did not wish."

"It is j-ju-just as well with me. I never th-thought to marry myself. But it seems the joining means a gr-gre-great deal to my father and our clan," replied Patrick.

"How so?"

"There is a considerable do-dow-dowry; and – the O'Malleys mean to con-construct a shipping port here and to pro-provide a vessel for my father."

"Of course. I can see your father's motivations." Airard rose and stood to place a hand on Patrick's shoulder. "Tell me son, what worries you the most?"

Patrick paused a moment in thought before responding. "I am f-f-fully trained as a blacksmith. I am ca-capable as a soldier. I can see to Br-Braeden's rearing."

"But?"

"Bbbb-but," stammered Patrick. "I know little of w-women. I have not the ca-capa-capacity to please a w-w-wife."

EIGHT

MacCahan Castle - Great Hall

"Patrick, I will be leaving for O'Malley lands shortly," spoke Ruarc over the morning meal in the great hall. Patrick's father nodded his approval from his seat at the high table.

"Deasum and Carbry will accompany you and Braeden on the road back and are bringing along two wagons for your things. Aengus is staying here for the time being, to begin construction on the piers."

Patrick grunted his approval and continued to eat grinning as he heard the familiar sound of Braeden snoring. He had fallen asleep on the bench next to Patrick, not accustomed to rising so early. The sun had not yet broken over the horizon.

"Patrick, can you be ready to leave in a few hours?" asked Ruarc.

"I b-b-believe so," replied Patrick. "I have only a few more things to gather and I w-w-wish to say goodbye to Airard."

"Do you think that Braeden will be able to sleep in the wagon?" Ruarc inquired as he chuckled.

"I think Braeden is able to sl-sleep through damn near anything," laughed Patrick as the sound of Braeden's snoring grew even louder.

Ruarc continued, "Riding alone, I should be able to arrive at the castle within at least three nights. I would guess your group should arrive within five to six nights at best, seeing you are bringing your belongings and you travel with Braeden."

Patrick set his mug down and scratched his head, nearly pulling the wisps of hair he had tied at the base of his neck from their hold. *I certainly hope it doesn't take longer than that – and that these infernal rains will stop. If we can't get through this mud, I'm not sure our belongings will make the trip.*

As if he understood his son's concerns, Breacan MacCahan interjected. "Patrick, I have instructed the men to pack tools for your trip and some extra wheels in the carts so that if you meet with any thick mud or rocks, you won't be stuck – you can continue your journey. You needn't worry about the carts."

"And," he continued, "We have fashioned the coverings over the wagons, so that the rain at least will not soak you through.

Your belongings will have some measure of covering, and the food is stored in clay pots that Glenia sealed for your journey."

"Thank you, f-f-father," replied Patrick. Turning to Ruarc, he inquired, "On your journey here, did it r-r-rain much?"

"Nay, we only encountered the weather when we arrived in MacCahan territory."

Thanks be. I do not think I can abide anymore storms. I feel like a drowned fish as it is. An entire day without drenching rain would be a blessing.

"Is there anything else along the jo-jou-journey we should keep watch for?" he asked Ruarc.

"Nay, except for the Burke lands," stated Ruarc. "But there is truly not much to worry about there either as long as you travel along the border and do it at night. They are woefully unprepared at night. Each of the other clans is aware of our quest and should cause you no ill. They will, of course, expect some coin for passage however," said Ruarc as he tilted his head towards Breacan.

"I see," interrupted Breacan. "Patrick I am sending you with plenty of resources; you needn't worry in that regard. "Carbry has been given charge of the coin being sent with you."

"Aye," laughed Carbry, "let me think where I put it," he said as he tugged at his beard with a menacing smile on his face. "Ah - there it 'tis" he said as he patted the satchel which was snuggly wrapped about his chest and laid just under his *bliaud*.

Ruarc drank the last remaining drops from his mug, finished off a final piece of bread and rose to gather his things. "My horse should be ready just about now. I must be off."

"Ru-Ruarc," interrupted Patrick. "I would like to have a w-wor-word. That is - I shall like to sp-sp-speak to you before you go, if you will?"

"Of course Patrick, let us walk," stated Ruarc, and the men headed out of the great hall and through the castle doors towards the path to the stables.

A flash of lightening in the morning sky was an instant reminder of the persistent storms that had surrounded the MacCahan keep for weeks. It hadn't yet begun to rain, but no doubt it would resume soon and Patrick needed to get moving before the ground again became saturated.

As they walked towards the stables, Patrick inquired. "Ruarc - what ma-ma-manner of woman may I ask is Da-Darina"?

"Darina is my niece, Patrick. She is the eldest daughter of Dallin and my sister, Anya. Both Dallin and Anya are deceased."

Patrick nodded his sympathies as Ruarc continued. "Darina is seventeen summers. She is by far one of the most unique lasses I have ever known. She possesses her father's keen intellect and her mother's beauty." Ruarc hesitated before saying, "She will make a fine wife, Patrick, she will."

"B-but," inquired Patrick, realizing something was being left unsaid.

"She has yet to grieve her parent's death Patrick. She has instead made herself her sister's keepers. At some point, I fear, the grief will come upon her and it will be difficult for her to hold back."

"I see," replied Patrick. "She is young, I am tw-tw-twenty-six summers; will she view me as an o-ol-old man?"

"I doubt that will be an issue," laughed Ruarc. "As long as you can keep up with her," he chuckled.

What is THAT supposed to mean? I've never had a problem keeping up with anyone. Patrick's face grew red instantly, from anger and humiliation.

"While I re-realize I am not whole," grunted Patrick raising both his voice and his right hand, "I am no weakling."

"Hold on, hold on Patrick," smiled Ruarc. "I did not mean to imply you are lacking in any way, at least in no way that is relevant."

Patrick let out a long audible sigh at Ruarc's words.

"Patrick," Ruarc continued shaking his head, "Darina is terribly quick witted. She has a sharp tongue and she is a fiercely competent opponent when it comes to the games. She is well skilled in archery and handy with a sword and axe. She is also a very fine hunter - and the best falconer I know; and she enjoys sparring more than any lad I have ever trained."

Patrick gasped and sneered in confusion. *A lass? Skilled with a sword? And she is permitted to spar?*

Ruarc gave Patrick a knowing look. "Our ways are not your ways Patrick. All the women in O'Malley territory are trained to defend themselves. Our lands are situated on the coast near the shipping lanes and we have all manner of merchants and visitors at any given time. It was only fitting that we ensure the safety of all of our clan."

"I see," replied Patrick, nodding his understanding.

"So," hesitated Ruarc. "So long as you can enjoy a contest, I see no reason you and Darina shall not get along finely."

"As long as I'm wi-wil-willing to spar with her?" Patrick asked mockingly. "Nay," replied Ruarc, "so long as you are willing to indulge her competitiveness."

"I see," laughed Patrick. "And - what else of her Ruarc?"

"Let's see, hmmm, what else should you know?" teased Ruarc, stroking his wiry beard. "Ah - she looks just like me!"

Patrick's face grew white as snow as he examined Ruarc head to toe. Ruarc was a man of slight stature, rotund with frizzy red hair and a course beard that fell to his chest. He barely met Patrick at his chest.

At the sight of Patrick's face, Ruarc let out a howl and clutched his sides as he bent over - he was laughing so hard. "You should see your face, my boy," belted Ruarc. "I jest with ye, I jest; I swear it is so!"

Patrick let out a cold, deep breath and the color returned to his face. "Thank the gods, Darina looks just like her dear mother. She has long golden red hair and crystal green eyes. She is tall for a lass, comes nigh to your chin Patrick, I would say." Patrick raised a suddenly interested eyebrow waiting for more.

"I *am* her Uncle, you know?" Ruarc stated guarding Patrick's reaction. "She is shapely though and has caught the eyes of many a suitor. You shan't be disappointed - Patrick. She is a beautiful one."

"Thank you, I just h-ho-hope she finds me suitable."

"After the way I have watched the lasses croon after you the past few days, I should say she won't have an issue," replied Ruarc. Patrick blushed, unsure if he had heard Ruarc correctly or not.

"Well, my son, I must be off," said Ruarc as he grabbed hold of his horse and prepared to mount.

"W-wait a moment," said Patrick. "Before you go, I have something, a g-gi - a present for Darina, if you don't m-m-mind."

Patrick handed him a blue velvet pouch which was laced with exquisite gold ribbon. "I wish for her to ha-ha-have this."

"May I?" inquired Ruarc, gesturing towards the ties. "Of course," Patrick said. Ruarc carefully untied the gold ribbon and opened the pouch. Inside the lush velvet lay an intricately detailed golden hair pin inlaid with rubies and sapphires. Attached on either side of the hair pin were lengths of blue ribbon intertwined with gold silken strands.

Ruarc gasped. "Patrick, wherever did you find such a priceless treasure?"

"'Twas my *mathair's*," replied Patrick. "Darina should have it n-no-now, as my betrothed."

"She will love it," came Ruarc's reply as he wrapped the pouch closed and placed it securely in his satchel.

"I am off now," said Ruarc as he mounted his horse and turned to leave. The sound of thunder echoed in the distance and the sun began to rise.

"Godspeed," said Patrick, "and a safe journey to you."

NINE

O'Malley lands - Roundhouse Quarters

Kyra was exhausted. *Every bone in my body aches, even my teeth hurt. If I never place my backside on another horse, I shall be most grateful.*

Nearly seven days had passed since she left the clan, and she was back already. *To deliver a one line message. What a waste of effort and horse flesh.*

As she sank down into the warm water that filled the wooden tub she wondered if she would be able to hold her head above the water long enough to properly wash. The warm bath was perfect and Minea had added bath salts and lavender oil and it smelled divine.

"Minea, I can't thank you enough for drawing my bath. I am sure I smell like a soggy war horse right about now." Minea chuckled and stole a glance towards Kyra's bed, which had become home to her muddy chain mail, cloak and undergarments.

80

"Do you wish that I should burn these Kyra? I fear they shall never come clean again," she said as she held them up in her right hand while pinching her nose with her left.

"Please do – I've no desire to ever see them again. And – I shall thrash my brother Kean the very next time I see him for getting himself hurt and making me journey all the way to MacCahan keep."

"Now Kyra, I'm sure that Kean did not have you in mind when he fell from the dock. He simply got his foot caught in the ropes and ended up on his arse on the pier. Or – so I am told."

"Minea – it is no secret that he was simply looking for a way to stay home with his young wife. A broken foot indeed; I'll believe it when I see it. Kean has spent the whole of his life searching for ways to have others do his bidding. I got wrangled into this one because it was his plan."

"Kyra, will you be taking a meal in your chambers? If so, I better head to the kitchens before the soldiers eat up all the remnants from this eve."

"Yes, please – and also – please see that I am not disturbed. I wish to sleep past sunrise in the morn, and I have no intention of breaking my fast with the others. Father has not returned and there is no one else that should have need of me."

Kyra reached across the top of the steaming tub of water to reach the soap and cleansing linens. She didn't think she could get all the grime out of her hair by herself, but she meant to try. *Thank the stars my hair is not long. One bar of soap might not be enough.*

"If that is all Kyra, I will make my way to the kitchens."

"Thank you so much Minea, could you see that some extra wood for the fire is brought up before I retire? I don't wish to wake up too cold."

"Very well - I will see to it," replied Minea as she headed out the door.

Kyra patiently ran her fingers through her matted hair which was stuck to the sides of her head. She had no idea what she looked like, but she could guess. *I'm sure I'm a sight. Now would not be a good time to venture outside of my chamber, I'm sure I would frighten six lives off of any tom cat around.*

Kyra finally succeeded in breaking apart the last pieces of matted hair and sunk deeper into the water, covering her head, her cheeks and finally her nose when she heard a loud ruckus coming from outside her chamber doors.

"I WILL see her Minea; just you try and stop me!"

By the stars, Darina knows I am here. I don't need this right now, I just need to sleep. She continued to hold her breath as if she could force time to stand still around her.

She heard the door creaking behind her and could sense someone in her room. She wasn't sure if Darina knew she was there in the tub until she felt someone grabbing her arm and pulling her straight up out of the water.

"Kyra, you'll drown yourself. Did you know you were asleep?" Darina flailed her hand about sending water flying everywhere.

Kyra inhaled deeply hoping to catch her breath but only succeeded in choking herself. Soon she was leaning over the side of the tub, heaving and hoping not to wretch. When her coughing and hacking finally subsided, she turned towards Darina.

"Darina, I wasn't trying to drown myself, if that is what concerns you."

"Of course not, I just assumed you were tired and that you had fallen asleep. You knew I couldn't wait until morning. You must tell me everything."

Darina must it be now? I really have nothing to tell you that you don't already know.

Darina reached to the peg on the side of the hearth and grabbed the drying linen for Kyra.

"Here, you'll catch your death if you don't get into some dry clothes soon. Minea is bringing up your dinner and I brought your favorite ale." Darina reached into her boot and brought out a small skin of ale.

"I'll let you get dressed, then we will talk, Kyra," and with that, Darina left.

* * *

Patrick said his last goodbyes to friends and family and gathered the final chests which held him and Braeden's belongings to be loaded onto the wagons. He had just settled Braeden down in the back of the wagon and covered him with a blanket when he heard the sound of a woman shouting.

"Patrick, Patrick! Wait," shouted Mavis. "Laird MacCahan says I am to accompany you. I had to get my things." Patrick looked up to see Mavis struggling with a large satchel which was obviously overstuffed as she climbed up the muddy path towards the castle gates.

By the time she crested the small hill, Mavis was out of breath and about to drop her satchel in the mud. Patrick quickly tied off the horses and rose to meet her on the hill.

"Mavis, let m-m-me have that," Patrick said as he pointed towards her bag. "What is this about you coming w-w-wi-ith us?"

"Laird MacCahan says I am to accompany you. I am Braeden's nurse after all and I came from O'Malley lands. He thinks it's time for me to return since that is where Braeden and you will be. I'm sure I can be of some use to you during the journey, don't you think?" she inquired as she glanced towards the back of the wagon where Braeden lay sleeping.

"I'm sure you will", chuckled Patrick. *Thank you father.*

"Here – take off your muddy sh-shoes and I will put you in the w-w-wa-wagon with Braeden."

"Nay – I'd much prefer to ride up front if you don't mind as I am in no mood to share a bed with Braeden - the way he snores." Mavis shared a knowing look with Patrick and stepped into the front of the wagon to sit next to him on the bench.

"Do you mind if I ride with you? I haven't a horse of my own."

"Not at all - j-ju-just as long as you don't snore."

Patrick grabbed the reins and signaled to Carbry that they were ready to go. Lightening flashed across the sky and a thunder clap followed. *There will be no reprieve for our journey, I fear.*

He handed his cloak to Mavis and gestured for her to cover her head as Braeden tussled about in the back but quickly fell back to sleep. "Tis a good thing he sleeps," said Mavis. "Such a journey can be quite hard on a child."

Patrick nodded his agreement and the group traveled out of the castle gates and on to the path heading southeast towards O'Malley lands. It would indeed be a long journey. One that Patrick hoped they would survive without incident.

TEN

Burke Lands

Cynbel Burke had grown inpatient waiting on his sister Odetta, to arrive. She had a knack for trying his resolve and he was sure she did it on purpose. He paced back and forth in the front of the altar of the monastery that Odetta had claimed as her own when she ran off the monks.

Odetta had turned the main chapel area into her own meeting hall and the remaining chambers and sitting rooms were now her private home. She resided in the only second story chamber while her "clerics" resided below on the first floor and saw to her every need.

"She will come. She insisted we meet her here and she will remain true to her word, my Laird." Easal McAllister was not only the one true friend of Cynbel Burke, but also captain of his soldiers. "I've no reason to believe she will not keep her word. I just wish I understood what all of this is about," remarked Easal.

"When did she say should we be here?" Cynbel asked Naelyn, her high cleric and personal servant.

"As I've already said my Laird; the noon hour. She indicated the noon hour. The meal is ready and will be served shortly. Just have a seat and she will come when she is ready."

"Naelyn, do you know? Where did she go?" questioned Easal.

"She went for herbs and roots, as is her custom on sunny days such as this. She is replenishing her stores for the great service."

"Ah - by the stars! The great service. You cannot mean to tell me that she still intends to go through with it? What utter nonsense. She has called me here to involve me in one of her ridiculous rituals," stated Cynbel as he threw his hands up in disgust over having his time wasted.

"I wouldn't go so far as to call it nonsense my brother. Would you Easal?" questioned Odetta as she strode into the hall.

Odetta Burke was a most conspicuous looking woman. Attractive - in the broadest sense of the word. She was tall and slender, with waist length onyx black hair and eyes of the darkest night. She held herself as royalty and commanded attention with her mere presence. She appeared much younger than her thirty-eight summers and had no want for male companionship. In fact, she had taken many of her clerics to her chamber and had what was rumored to be an insatiable appetite for love making.

"Easal, what did you say?" she queried. "I said, of course not. Of course not. It's not nonsense. Your special talents have meant much to the Burke clan."

"Oh hush, won't you Easal? You only say that because you wish to share her bed," exclaimed Cynbel. *Which I'm sure you have already and on many occasions.*

"Odetta, what do you need with me?" asked Cynbel. "I have many other, more important matters to attend to."

"More important than the expansion of Burke lands?" asked Odetta. "More important than the size of your realm? More important than the people over whom you rule? More important than our dominion? More important than the great service?"

"Odetta, for many years I have over looked your religious dabbling's. I have turned my head when you orchestrated and manipulated situations with your craft. I even indulged your desire to run off the monks and let you take their monastery – while the villagers watched with dismay."

"Stop it!" shouted Odetta and threw her fist against the altar. "Hear me now, my brother. You do not wish to cross me. If it were not for me, you would not be Laird of Burke lands. As it stands, I have more respect from the people and more power than you ever will. Do not tempt me to replace you too," she smiled as she gestured a glance towards Easal.

"Easal would make a fine husband and if I marry, my husband would no doubt be Laird in your absence. That is – if you should meet with some unfortunate occurrence. Lest you forget what happened to our sister," said Odetta.

"Odetta! Enough already!" shouted Cynbel. "What is it you want from me?"

"Laird O'Malley has passed and his wife as well." stated Odetta.

"How do you know this?" asked Easal.

"I have my ways Easal. I know of all of the goings on in the O'Malley clan. What we need to concentrate on now is how to overtake the clan and make O'Malley port a part of the Burke lands."

"And just why would I want to do that?" asked Cynbel.

"Because you are just as opportunistic as I am; because you want to expand your reach and because it will bring us great wealth. Combining what's left of the O'Malley clan with the Burkes would make us the most significant power in all of Ireland."

"Because - we would be unstoppable," chimed in Easal.

"Tell me what you are thinking. What is going on in the beautiful head of yours Odetta?" asked Easal as he approached Odetta and laid a hand on either side of her cheeks.

Odetta smiled. She smiled because she knew she could make Easal do whatever she wanted; because she knew her brother didn't stand a chance at denying her what she wanted. It hadn't worked for her sister and it wouldn't work for Cynbel.

Soon it would all be hers.

* * *

Kyra awoke at the knock on her door. She knew who it was and there was no escaping it. Darina had questions, and she somehow, would have to offer her answers.

"Thanks for seeing me, Kyra. I realize you are tired, but you must understand my concerns. I have not a clue what is happening. Your father ignored my pleas for information and you both took off to MacCahan castle in such a rush, that I feared the worst. Please tell me, won't you, what is going on?"

Darina crossed the threshold of Kyra's chambers and sat beside her on the bed. She grabbed the comb on the chest next to her and began to comb through Kyra's wet, tangled hair.

"Honestly, Darina. I don't know much at all. When your father passed, I was asked to fetch Lucian. They told me to make sure he brought the clan registry."

"The registry? What on earth would they need that for?"

"Well I'm sure they needed to record the deaths of your parents, Darina. But there was something more."

"Tell me."

"I don't know. I'm not sure, I mean, I think I know but I'm not really positive."

"Oh by the stars - just spit it out Kyra."

"It appeared to be a manuscript. Perhaps a dictate issued by your father - that looked to have been sealed for many years."

"His will perhaps?" asked Darina.

"I don't think so. You and I both went over his testament with Father MacArtrey after his death. This was definitely not the same manuscript."

"I see. What then?" asked Darina.

"I'm not sure. All I know is that I was asked to ride to MacCahan castle to announce the arrival of father and his men and to return at once."

"But, you took a message. Did you not?"

"Yes I did."

"Well?"

"Well what?"

"Well – what did it say Kyra?"

"It said, 'It is time'," answered Kyra with a reluctant sigh.

"It is time? It is time? That's all it said? What is that supposed to mean?"

"I have no idea Darina. I really wish I could tell you something that might make some sense of all of this. But I can't. I haven't any idea what all of this is about. And I'm halfway sure it has nothing, at all, to do with your upcoming wedding."

Darina rose from the bed and walked towards the fireplace. She shook her head in confusion and placed one hand on the mantle as if wishing it would hold her up. *I've never fainted before, and I'm not about to start now. Breathe. Breathe. I'm sure this will all make sense when Ruarc returns.*

"Thank you Kyra, you have been most helpful. I won't intrude on your rest any longer. We can speak more tomorrow. I should be getting to bed myself and it's past my curfew. Your father would have my head if he knew I wasn't at the castle."

"Don't you wish to ask me about Him?" inquired Kyra.

"Him? Him who?" replied Darina.

"Your betrothed Darina - Patrick MacCahan."

"Patrick. Patrick is his name?" asked Darina.

"Yes it is."

"Well of course, tell me what you know then."

"Not much actually. I only saw him for a brief time. I wasn't there more than an hour in total I believe."

"And?"

"He is very handsome. He is a tall man with the body of an experienced warrior. A solid jaw line, long brown hair he keeps tied at the back of his neck, green eyes. A true highlander, from what I could see."

"Sounds like you got a good enough look Kyra," laughed Darina.

"Well - I tell you he was hard to miss," retorted Kyra. "If he is half as accommodating in the bed a he is handsome, you shall stay busy for quite some time after your wedding I perceive," she gushed.

"Kyra, you are so unseemly," laughed Darina. "I'm sure I have no idea what you are talking about."

"Oh don't play the prude with me Darina. I know as well as anyone that you have taken lovers before. I know you have gone to the Women's Island during the Lunar Bacchanals on many occasions. Don't pretend you are innocent. There is no need. Although I'm sure none of the men would tell; I know we could find one or two around here who have known you too."

"Kyra, you are so exhausted you are delirious," signed Darina. "I will see you on the morrow."

ELEVEN

Burke Lands – Odetta's Monastery

"Naelyn, bring me the great scrolls," shouted Odetta from her chamber.

Odetta was in one of her moods. Dark, angry and ready for a fight. Naelyn knew better than to make Odetta wait, so she rushed down to the library to find the great scrolls. No doubt Odetta was searching for one of her spells or curses and this could only mean one thing. *Trouble.*

"Here you go my lady."

"Good now find me the curse I cast over the O'Malley sons. It should be somewhere in the beginning."

Naelyn laid the scrolls down on top of the high table which sat under the eastern facing window and began to unroll the pages. She shuffled through page after page of ancient markings and symbols, careful not to tear or crumple any of the parchments. After she had gone through the rolls one at a time for the second time, she grew hesitant.

"Odetta, it's not here!"

"What do you mean - it's not there?" echoed Odetta.

"I've looked through all of the pages, and I don't see it. This volume only goes back for fifteen years, Odetta. We cast that spell over twenty years ago. Did the scribe record it?"

"He better have," came her reply.

"Easal, thank the gods, you are just the man I need," said Odetta tipping her head to him as he walked through the doorway and towards the high table.

Easal blushed as he walked into the chamber to greet Odetta. *Well I certainly hope you feel that way* - he thought to himself - *especially after last night.*

"Easal, I have need of the scribe. Naelyn has been unable to locate the original curse in the great scrolls and I must consult with him at once. There is much to be done and much planning for the great service, and I have need for it."

"Cynbel will be none too happy if I leave Burke lands, you know this Odetta. Besides, we have been on high alert since you imprisoned the merchant. Have you yet to determine what is to become of him?"

Odetta stood from her chair by the fire and walked towards Easal. She had the look of a lover in her eyes, and Easal grew more aroused the closer she came. Just remembering their time together the night before caused him to gasp with anticipation of what was to come. No doubt she hadn't drunk her fill and would want him again.

And so soon. Naelyn, leave. Leave, he thought. *We don't need your interruption now.* He glared at Naelyn with squinted eyes and motioned for her to be dismissed. But Naelyn didn't budge. She glared back before continuing her search through the mound of papers.

Odetta swayed her luscious hips in a rhythmic fashion and held her head high as she grew close to Easal. She stopped just in front of him to survey his form. *It is nice indeed.* When she lifted her chin to look him in the eye, she knew he was hers. He would do her bidding; there was not even a question of it. She licked her lips and Easal grew hard with anticipation. When she raised her arms towards him, he let out a long breath of expectancy and waited.

Odetta's hand struck hard against his cheek. The sting of
the connection forced him backwards, stumbling towards the
floor. He raised an arm and braced himself against the wall,
holding his jaw. When Naelyn looked up, she could clearly see
the outline of Odetta's hand on Easal's face, red, white and
beginning to swell.

"You should focus on what I plan to do with *you* Easal.
Forget the merchant and stop questioning me. I do not answer to
you or my brother. You know this!"

"Yes my lady," said Easal still rubbing his cheek.

"Now - bring me the scribe."

"But..."

"But what Easal? But what?"

"I'll have to clear it with Cynbel, if I am to go to
O'Malley territory."

"I'll clear it with it Cynbel. You just go!"

* * *

Darina hadn't slept at all the previous night. After her
conversation with Kyra, she was even more confused and dismayed.
Surely when Ruarc arrived he would have more information or at
least some guidance for her. Her future and that of her clan was

in question, and the port merchants were also counting on a secure alliance and security of the port to continue their trading.

But that wasn't what troubled Darina the most. Kyra had mentioned that she knew Darina had attended the Lunar Bacchanal celebrations. Although Darina was aware that most of the young women in the O'Malley clan had participated at least once in the monthly festivals on the Women's island, she hadn't been sure that Kyra or her sisters knew. She had hoped they hadn't.

Tis just as well. At least my betrothed won't see me as a prudish virgin. After all, times have changed. And the clan's women had been celebrating the Lunar Bacchanals for years. Just what else is a woman to do? There are no men to be had around here.

Over the last two decades, most of the young unmarried women of the clan had taken up residence on the closer of the two islands which sat just off the western side of the port. It had become home to several hundred women who pooled their resources together and took care of each other. The island itself offered a form of shelter and safety from unwelcome visitors as one could only get there by boat.

There were ten large round houses on the island with one main fortress that resembled a small castle. Most of the women resided in the castle, while the round houses were kept for visitors and soldiers stationed to protect the island against invaders.

Each month, at the full moon, the women of the island held a festival and opened their docks to guests to celebrate the Lunar Bacchanal. There was feasting and dancing, musicians and story tellers and large bonfires that could be seen from the High Castle on the mainland. The festival itself typically ran for two nights, beginning on the eve of the full moon.

The Lunar Bacchanal festival was a tribute to their goddess Morrigan and celebrated the importance of fertility and war. The women would create elaborate head coverings made of crow feathers and dance and sing in sensual unity in preparation for the sacred joining's to come.

It was a night of magical harmony and enticement. At midnight each invited man would be chosen by a woman or group of women to share their bodies and their beds to partake in the worship of Morrigan and in hopes of conceiving a child. Many children had been born of the Bacchanals, but never a male. Somehow the curse that Odetta had placed on the clan had also reached the Island of Women.

As far as Darina knew, Kyra had never been to a Bacchanal celebration. Darina had attended on more than one occasion and while she quite enjoyed the dancing and feasting and gaiety of the entire event, her experience with the men was not what she had hoped.

The festivals themselves were spell-binding. Gemma - who had been stewardess of the island since as long as Darina could remember - made sure of that. It was unlike anything anyone had ever seen. From the wine, which flowed freely, to the elaborate meal with exotic foods - Gemma left nothing out. The women of the island dressed in their most provocative attire taking great pains to look their best. Many would spend hours adorning each other's hair and wearing only the finest jewels they had.

From an outsider's standpoint, it resembled something close to a Roman orgy. The ladies entertained and the men were waited upon as if they were kings. At the large feast table, it was not uncommon to witness a solider being hand fed by three or four different women.

The air was filled with sensuous wonder and unexpected delight. Indeed the Lunar Bacchanal was a festival unlike any other. Darina had loved the feasting and dancing, and had even looked forward to the coupling at midnight. But not anymore. Gemma told her it was "simply unfortunate your partner for the evening was not skilled in the ways of loving - especially since it was your first time."

Although Darina had enjoyed the wooing and kissing enough; her partner had scarcely any patience and way too much ale. It had ended as abruptly as it had begun and left her feeling used and unwanted. She had sworn to herself after that day that she would never again share her bed with a man. Gemma had been a comfort however; and had somehow even convinced her to return to the feasts - on more than one occasion - although she had never again selected a partner at midnight.

Tales of the O'Malley lands Lunar Bacchanal had traveled throughout all of Ireland. Many a man had come seeking admittance to the festival only to be turned away. In fact, many of the hired soldiers had arrived in O'Malley territory specifically to seek out the Festival.

But - over the years it had become more than a routine gathering for a sensual escape. Several fine matches had been made between the invited guests and women of the island. Several marriages had resulted and the clan grew bigger. Gemma had maintained the religious origins of the Festival and kept the rites as they had been handed down; much to the chagrin of Father MacArtrey.

Since the day he had become the clan's priest, Father MacArtrey had made every plausible attempt to stop the monthly festivals. Denouncing it as "evil imbibing's" and "the devil's doorway" he had received little support from the local men in changing the tradition. Even Laird O'Malley was hard pressed to change the custom as he had met his beloved Anya at one such festival.

Father MacArtrey continued to offer his services at the chapel and maintained his ministry amongst the poor, sick and grieving, but he and Dallin had clashed over the years over many matters. Laird O'Malley was not accustomed to being told what to do, nor would he allow his people to be burdened with the "guilt of religion" as he put it.

For that reason, Darina had always looked at Father MacArtrey with doubting eyes. *There is something about him that I do not trust.*

Besides his desire to control every aspect of the lives of the clan's people, Father MacArtrey was constantly in the know – about everything. He was involved it seemed, in every birth, death, pregnancy, illness or incident. He had so angered the clan healer that she had left O'Malley lands and they were forced to commission a healer from another territory. Lucian had had his fill of the priest years before, when he found him rummaging through the registry and clan manuscripts in his

cottage. From that day on; Deasum - the second in command over

the clan warriors - had set a sentry to keep watch over the

priest.

TWELVE

Central Ireland - the Journey toward O'Malley Lands

Patrick awoke to the sound of soft whispers outside the tent he shared with Braeden. He had only been asleep a short while as he had taken the first watch. The patch of trees along the stream had hidden their camp well enough to host a fire for the evening and he could hear the wood crackling and smell a stew that was left over from their evening meal.

"You should have told us. All these years, and you said nothing?" asked Carbry loudly. "I should thrash you for this. Do you realize how much danger you have put us in, and the child?"

Who on earth is he talking to and what about? When heard the sound of faint sobbing, Patrick knew his sleeping was over.

Deasum spoke next, "Carbry, exactly what would ye have had her do? She had no other choice, the way I see it. I would have probably done the same thing."

"Please forgive me, I only wanted to help the child after my daughter perished, and I - when you took me from the slave traders, I felt I owed you," said Mavis.

Great stars, now I'll have to get up and see what this is about. Patrick rose from the tent, put his cloak on and joined the others around the fire. It was apparent that Mavis had been sobbing quite a while and Carbry looked like he was ready to kill someone. Deasum had stepped between them in an attempt to mediate the matter.

"Whatever is the f-fu-uss?" inquired Patrick to Mavis.

Mavis hung her head in shame. "Patrick, I haven't exactly been honest with you or your family. I have hidden something from you of great importance. Not out of malice, mind you, but I did it nonetheless. Carbry wishes to see me punished for my error."

"Ca-Car-Carbry, what is this about?" directed Patrick.

"Let me," replied Deasum and put a hand in front of Carbry to keep him where he was. "Mavis, please return to your tent, all will be well."

107

"Yes, my lord," she replied and rose and stepped away.

"Patrick, please have a seat. I will do the best I can to explain this to you."

Patrick nodded and reclined on a fallen log and began stoking the fire with a walking stick, sending smoke and sparks upwards.

"Patrick, when we came to MacCahan castle with Braeden - do you remember that?"

"Aye."

"We brought Mavis with us."

"Aye."

"Did your father ever explain the circumstances involving Mavis, to your knowledge?" asked Deasum.

"Nay, I don't b-b-be-believe so."

"Well then. Let me. Patrick, Braeden was born in the O'Malley castle, he is the son of the Laird, the youngest child. They already had 5 daughters. Many years before, Odetta Burke, the eldest daughter of the neighboring laird, placed a curse on the O'Malley clan such that they would not bear any male children. Over the years, any male children to be found on

O'Malley lands were kidnapped, sold as slaves or killed by the Burkes."

"You b-b-believe in curses?" asked Patrick.

"It does not matter what I believe, Laird O'Malley feared for the safety of his son. Carbry and I were instructed to bring the child to MacCahan castle to Monae for keeping. But he was such a wee bairn, we had no way to feed him, and he would not take to the goat's milk," he replied.

"G-go on."

"So we stopped in MacLeod territory on the way and passed by a slave auction," interjected Carbry.

"Mavis was a young woman who had been sold into slavery, and she had recently birthed a child who did not live. We bought her freedom so she could become a nurse to Braeden. She agreed to accompany us to MacCahan lands – she was not forced."

"I see," replied Patrick. "And wh-what is she so upset about?"

"Well, it seems she is terrified to cross through the Burke territory."

"And wh-why is that?"

"She lied to us," grunted Carbry through clenched teeth.

Deasum held out his hand toward Carbry in a sign to be quiet. He continued, "She wasn't completely honest with us. You see, Braeden hadn't even a name when we left the territory; we let her name the child. He became Braeden Cordal McTierney, after her husband Cordal McTierney."

"Wh-where is her husband?" asked Patrick.

"She doesn't know, but she believes he may have been sold into slavery as well. But that's not the point."

"It's not?"

"No - the point is that she lied about her identity."

"She is not Mavis McTierney?"

"Not exactly. She is the wife of Cordal McTierney, but her name is not Mavis."

"Who is sh-she?" gasped Patrick.

"She is Raelyn Burke."

"A B-Burke," gulped Patrick. As in 'The Burkes'?"

"Yes."

Carbry couldn't hold himself back any longer. The anger had risen in him to such a point he felt he would explode. His face grew red and dripped with sweat near his brow and his hands were twisted into fists he could not undo.

"She will be the death of us; we will never make it out of here alive with her in tow. We are walking into a trap," he said.

"Nay. Hold on Carbry, there is no need to get worked up; it can't be as bad as that. We will find a way," responded Deasum.

"I don't understand what the problem is," said Patrick.

"She is terrified, she has begged us not to take her through Burke lands, but there is no other way, except by boat, and we are three days ride out of the way from the nearest ship launch."

"She is a-af-afraid of her own home?"

"Yes, Patrick, it was her sister, Odetta, that sold her into slavery. Her brother, Cynbel, is the new Laird and he did nothing to stop this when it happened. Her parents presumed her dead," replied Carbry.

"Patrick, she has asked that we leave her here, on her own, but I cannot do that," said Deasum

"I see."

"But she is free to do as she chooses. She has never been a slave to us; we freed her the moment we paid her fees. She chose to accompany Braeden and has been with him ever since."

"She would rather be l-lef-left behind than tr-tr-travel through her own lands?"

"Yes."

"Unbelievable. What k-ki-kind of person is th-this, Odetta Burke?"

"The worst possible kind; she is an evil witch without a conscious or an ounce of simple humanity. She will stop at nothing to get what she wants. You see what she did to her own sister?"

"But what would have possessed her to do that to her own kin?"

"Mavis married her first love," came the reply.

"By the stars!" Patrick rose to pace the camp site.

"And when she heard that Mavis, I mean Raelyn was with child, she captured them both and held them in the dungeons. When the child was born, Odetta took it from her and sent Raelyn to the slave traders. She was later told the babe had perished."

"W-well I cannot permit her to remain behind. She must come with us, for her safety and for Braeden's sake," said Patrick. He rose and walked towards the entrance of Mavis' tent, the sound of cries still permeating the air.

"M-Mavis - will you come out here please?"

"Of course."

Mavis stepped through the opening in her tent and straightened herself before heading towards the fire. She wiped the tears from her cheek with the back of her hand and glared fiercely at Carbry from the other side of the fire.

"Please sit," said Deasum.

"Thank you."

"Mavis, it a-ap-appears we have a situation," said Patrick.

"Yes my lord."

"But I want you to be ve-ver-very clear about one thing."

"Aye."'

"We are in no w-way pu-punish-punishing you. No one here can blame you for what you ha-have done."

Carbry gasped and snorted and flung himself down on the log on his side of the campfire.

"Carbry will cause you no gr-gri-grief," he said as he shot a stern glance towards him. "And – he will have no-not-nothing more to say in the matter."

"Aye," came the reluctant reply of Carbry.

Patrick directed his gaze towards Mavis who had briefly stopped her sobbing.

"M-Mavis, do you trust me," asked Patrick.

She nodded yes in reply.

"You are always we-wel-welcome in my home, Mavis, wherever that may be. But I will not le-leave you here. You must come wi-with us to O'Malley lands."

Mavis erupted into mournful sobs and began shaking violently. Patrick rose to stand beside her and placed his hand upon her shoulder in comfort.

"Mavis, I will not let an-any-anything happen to you. When we arrive in O'Malley lands, you will be free to leave at any time. They have a shi-ship-shipping port there and I'm sure there are me-merchants who can take you wh-whe-wherever you would like to go."

Through clasped hands, Mavis nodded her acknowledgement.

"I will get y-you there safely. You have my word."

"Our word," interrupted Deasum, and Carbry nodded in agreement.

THIRTEEN

Burke Lands

It was nigh close to midnight and Easal had been travelling
for hours. Most of the O'Malley clan would either be retired to
their homes due to the curfew or celebrating the Lunar Bacchanal
on the island. It made it much easier to sneak into the
territory when the soldiers were otherwise occupied.

*He better be easy to find this time and bring his own
damned horse. I refuse to ride double with the man ever again.*
Just the thought made his skin crawl.

It had been nearly three fort nights since Odetta had sent
for the scribe. His presence was typically not required since
they had begun correspondence through the merchants. But Odetta
needed him to locate the curse on the O'Malley clan and since
her cleric could not, most likely the scribe could, since he
would have been the one to record it.

Easal knew that he could not return to the monastery without the scribe and he could not risk being found by the O'Malley's either. If the O'Malley's knew of the spy in their midst it would ruin all of Odetta's plans. *Tis a very good thing tonight is their feast. Even if I am found, they will presume me to be a guest here for the festival.*

Easal tied off his horse and snuck around the port side of the shore towards the path leading up to the inn. There was bustling activity even at such a late hour, as it had been a market day and many of the merchants were staying overnight. *Thank the stars I changed my clothing.* Easal had managed to obtain an O'Malley plaid and wore it over his tunic and truis. *This will be easier than I thought.*

He trudged up the winding path just passed the inn and behind the large section of trees, towards the chapel hidden in the outcrops. *There! I hope he's in.*

He made his way to the back of the small cottage behind the chapel and found the door ajar. A look inside told him he was in the right place. The stench of day old food and sour ale caught him in his nostrils. *Uh, but the man is a wretch!*

"MacArtrey! MacArtrey! Where are you, you lazy swine?" called Easal. There was barely enough light to see in the cottage and the fire had long since died, although there were still some gleaming red coals. Easal bent down near the hearth and had the fire going again, when he heard snoring and grumbling from the corner.

There sitting in the corner propped up against the wall on a three legged stool sat Father MacArtrey, half asleep and half drunk, as usual.

"MacArtrey, don't you hear me calling you?"

At that, the priest startled and tipped himself over landing squarely on the floor with a loud thud.

"Easal, my boy, what are you doing here?"

"Odetta has sent for you. She needs you immediately. We must go before I am found."

"I cannot go now. I am to attend to the wedding of Darina in four days' time."

"A wedding? What an interesting development. I'll let you tell Odetta all about it," replied Easal as he grabbed the priest by the nape of the neck and swung him back onto his feet. He swayed when he stood upright and looked to be about ready to empty his stomach when Easal grabbed him sternly about the face.

"Compose yourself man. You are a man of the cloth, yet you have too much of a liking for the spirits."

"A man of the cloth, my arse," replied MacArtrey. "I have been Odetta's puppet for too long. I should have let her kill me like the others when she claimed our monastery. Instead, I became her slave. I am no kind of a man!"

"You have the right of it," replied Easal - "Now let's go."

* * *

Aengus sat beside Laird MacCahan in the great hall, going over sketches and plans for the piers to be constructed for the port. There was plenty of food and merriment to be had as a celebration was underway to commemorate the coming nuptials of Patrick MacCahan and Darina O'Malley; a union which would no doubt result in much prosperity for each clan.

All that could be heard throughout the castle was the sound of men's laughter mingled with the harp and the pounding of dancing feet. "Come Airard, join us," said Laird MacCahan.

"I believe I will," he replied and pulled his legs up over the bench that sat across from Breacan's chair at the high table.

"How go the plans?" he asked.

"Very well. Very well indeed wouldn't you say, Aengus?"

"Yes, very well. We should like to begin construction in a fort night before winter sets in fully. We should have the main posts set first and wait until spring to set the others. In the meantime, we have several men finalizing plans for the first shipping vessel."

"Indeed it does go well then," replied Airard. "And what of Patrick? Have you had word of their arrival?" he asked the Laird.

"Nay, not as of yet. We didn't expect them to arrive until tomorrow eve as it stands."

"And what of the wedding? When do you expect they will be joined?" he inquired.

"Not for another eve or so after their arrival I presume," interjected Aengus. "I would expect he would want to get the lay of the land beforehand, and perhaps spend some time with his betrothed before they are joined."

"Yes, I would expect so," said Laird MacCahan.

"My laird, has Patrick been fully apprised of the situation and his role?" asked Airard.

"What do you mean?" asked Aengus.

Directing his attention to the Laird, Airard asked again. "Is Patrick *fully* aware of the situation?"

"Nay, not fully," said the Laird hesitantly while he mindlessly pushed the papers in front of him about on the table.

Aengus rose from his chair to pace in front of the hearth. "What do you mean, not fully? I sat with you in your chambers while we explained things to him. I don't get your meaning old man."

"Aye - 'tis so Aengus. We told him all that we could. But we did not warn him about what awaits him in Burke lands."

"We told him to be careful and watchful while traversing the lands, he was made aware," said Aengus.

"But we did not tell him of the other," replied the Laird. "That, I fear, he must find out on his own."

"Airard, I should ask you. Is he prepared even if he is not aware," asked the Laird.

"Aye, my lord. He is prepared. Of that, I have no doubt."

FOURTEEN

O'Malley Strong House

It was well past dusk when the guards alerted that a horseman was seen in the distance. "Call for Kyra," the watchman alerted. Quickly a young girl in work truis traveled down the winding stairs that led up to the towers and ran out the back entry of the castle towards the round house.

She stumbled clumsily through the door that lead to the dining hall and caught Minea's eye. "I must wake Kyra," she said to Minea through ragged breath. A rider is coming and she needs to intercept him. "Is she here?"

"I'm here," came the sound from the back of the kitchens. "How far out do you think he is?"

"He's just above the clearing on the peek. It shouldn't take more than half an hour to arrive, but it is getting dark."

"Does he wear a plaid?" asked Kyra.

"Nay. None that we can tell - because he is wearing a cloak."

Minea groaned and gave Kyra a hesitant look of concern.

"It may be my father, Minea," she said with a comforting stare.

Kyra turned to the girl and said, "Please, run and tell Moya to ready my horse. I'll go up and change and meet you at the stables."

Kyra grabbed the back of her shoulder length hair and tied it off as she ran up the stairs to her chambers to grab her helmet and chain mail. Thankfully she had finally caught up on her rest after returning from MacCahan territory, and a ride would be welcome. Although - she hoped she wouldn't meet with trouble.

It's probably just father returning early from his journey. Perhaps he will be luckier than I was and escape Darina's detection until the morrow. Kyra chuckled when she thought of it, knowing it would not be so.

***

It was her - the one with the big green eyes and haunting stare. Patrick watched her as she traversed the broken ground on the way to the cliff which over looked the river. She seemed in a hurry and kept looking behind her as if someone was chasing her. For a moment, he was sure she spotted him, hidden in the trees just down the path from the trail she had taken.

A flush came about her face and Patrick could see the tears stinging her cheeks and lapping about in her hair as the wind rose around her. Inch by inch she rose higher on the peek until she topped the cliff and turned to survey her lot.

She became frantic with panic and turned to look down at the rocks and cliffs below. The wind continued its assault upon her and her fiery golden red hair distorted his view of her as it overtook her face.

In the distance, the melancholy cry of a falcon seeking its prey grew closer. Closer, closer it circled towards her. It dipped down almost as if to touch her and then it rose again. She sunk to her knees and reached to grip the stones below the cliff. They loosened and fell below the rocky tips.

She has nowhere to go.

She rose again and turned to address a faceless enemy. *What is she saying? I can't quite hear her.*

The falcon screeched a forlorn warning and circled again. *By the stars, she is going to jump!* Patrick shouted into the wind, but she couldn't hear him. She backed further and further towards the edge. He was sure the wind would take her over.

What is she looking at?

Patrick turned and saw her enemy. A black haired woman and two men were growing closer to her and she continued to edge closer to the cliff. One of the men raised a bow and pointed it towards her.

A distinct look of terror overtook her as she fell to her knees again. The falcon circled and dove towards her just as the arrow was released.

"No!" cried Patrick as he ran towards the cliff.

"No!"

"Patrick! Patrick!"

Strong arms gripped his shoulders and shook him violently. "Patrick!" it continued. "He can't hear me. He won't wake up," said the voice.

"Patrick! You must wake up," said a feminine voice.

He floated there just above the trees, watching the scene below him unfold. The falcon continued its descent as Patrick rose above the trees into the fog that covered the mountain tops. He reached for her, but she was gone. The terror in her eyes etched forever in his memory.

A dull pain erupted in the back of his head and rained shivers down the base of his neck. He felt heavy. So. Heavy.

His eyelids refused to budge and the ringing in his ears grew worse as he began to recognize something. Somewhere. Someone.

"Patrick," it came at him again.

"Patrick! Please wake up."

In a flash, his eyes were wide and his head felt as if it had been split clean in two.

Braeden.

He felt the familiar grip of sweat soaked bed linens wrapped about his legs and struggled for air. The scent of burning pine and woods lingered in his nostrils and he sat upright.

"Patrick, thanks be to the gods, you're awake," came Mavis' hesitant voice.

Deasum entered the tent and lurched over Patrick's near lifeless form. "Patrick, are you alright?"

"Aye."

"You nearly scared the leaves off the trees man. We thought you were being attacked."

"A bear," shouted Braeden. "They had no idea what was wrong. Until I told them it was nothing but your night terrors. 'Tis best they get used to them? Aye - Patrick?" he asked.

Patrick nodded and wiped the sweat from his brow with the back of his hand. He could see the stars from his tent and knew it was well into the night and almost morn. He had woken the entire camp.

"Give me a m-mo-moment, please. I'll be out in a sh-short time," he said to Carbry giving him a look that conveyed both comfort as well as irritation.

"Go on," Patrick nodded towards Braeden.

"I'll warm you some porridge," he heard Mavis say as she sauntered back towards the roaring fire.

"Braeden, what of these night terrors of Patrick's?" questioned Carbry as he arose from his tent to step before the fire.

"Carbry, 'tis none of your concern," shot Deasum from the other side of the fire.

"'Tis common place with Patrick," interjected Mavis as she stood over the fire, stirring the oats. "He's had these night terrors since the very moment I met him. You should grow quite used to them if you intend to safeguard your new laird."

Braeden stretched and laid his legs out in front of the fire after setting down upon the log in front of Patrick's tent. "Patrick has his night terrors almost every night," he said, matter-of-factly.

"But I calm him well enough."

"Aye, Braeden has brought him much comfort over the years." said Mavis as she smiled.

"Is there nothing to be done?" asked Deasum.

"Nay, all has been tried. Even sleeping elixirs and resting herbs have done naught for him."

"What are they about?" asked Carbry.

Braeden interjected before Mavis or Deasum could stop him.

"'Tis about his mother," he said.

"Aye," came the sound from Patrick's tent.

Patrick rose from his tent and joined the others in front of the fire; a look of interrupted sleep adorned his face and he rubbed his arms in hopes of crushing the chill that had come upon them.

"'Twas not about my mathair th-though," her offered.

"What?" gasped Mavis.

"Nay," he replied. "'Twas about the strange lass again."

"Strange lass?" asked Carbry with an inquisitive stare. "Tell us Patrick, what have you dreamed this night?"

"Nay," retorted Deasum. "There is no need; it is none of our concern."

"It's a bad omen, I tell you. We must know what he has seen," retorted Carbry.

"It's j-ju-just a silly dream," replied Patrick. "B-but I will tell you."

FIFTEEN

Burke Lands – Odetta's Monastery

The chanting grew louder. The sound of what seemed a million voices rose in the air and mingled with the musty scent of fresh rain and autumn grass. The circle had grown larger and threatened to breech the entry doors; nearly all her disciples were there. It wouldn't be long and she would have every last one of them.

Odetta raised her arms in the midst of her coven and bellowed, "The time is near." The chanting turned to humming; a deep ominous sound - the mixture of voices and magic. Crackling fire wood splintered in two and filled the chamber with smoke, thick and electric.

Naelyn stood in the midst of the smoke near the hearth and opened the great scroll to read aloud.

"In the tenth moon, under raven skies;

The King will emerge and take a bride.

A kingdom secured, a people oppressed

With infinite power a king possessed."

A sacred hush flooded the gathering and an eerie chill wound its way through the crowd, stopping to rest atop Naelyn as she closed the great scroll and ceremoniously laid it on the mantle. A startled cry echoed behind the group as a ruckus entered the hall, a mixture of surprise and disbelief.

Easal trudged forward towards the hearth while Cynbel followed closely behind, a small boy in tow. A brief look of astonishment took over Naelyn's face and she moved to join the others in the congregation as she stepped from the platform facing the hearth.

"Here is your sacrifice, my lady," said Cynbel mockingly, as he shoved the boy towards Odetta and the altar. A young boy, no older than perhaps eight winters, tripped as he rose towards Odetta near the altar. A look of terror and confusion apparent on his tear stained cheeks as he rubbed his freshly shaven head and spoke.

"What do you intend to do with me?" he whimpered.

"I intend to offer you to the gods as a token of our loyalty and respect," said Odetta.

"And what will killing me do for you?" he asked bravely and with a defiant lip.

"You ask too many questions," she retorted.

* * *

Kyra mounted her horse and whispered her goodbyes to Moya as she exited the stables. The sun was going down quickly and she needed to intercept whoever was riding towards the keep before it became too dark to see. As she rounded the path towards the outer gates she heard a comforting familiar sound.

The shrill cry of Darina's falcon, Riann became louder the closer Kyra came to the exterior walls of the castle. She could barely make out her shape as she flew circles around the bay under the backdrop of the setting sun. But there was no mistaking her call. As if she sensed her presence, Riann raised high and riding the wind, wound her way down towards the lone rider.

"You'll have company this eve," said the sentry as Kyra grew closer to the outer gate.

"It appears I will."

"No doubt it is your father, I presume. Else Riann would have warned us already."

"Of that I'm sure," said Kyra as she motioned for the guards to begin turning the gate wheels. "Of that I'm sure, indeed."

Unable to contain her curiosity, and dissatisfied with the limited view afforded by the arrow slit windows in her chamber - Darina quickly dressed and headed down the stairs towards the castle doors.

"My lady, what are you off to in so much haste?" inquired Odhran, the castle bailiff, from the fireplace in the great hall.

"Riann is loose again and signaling an approaching rider. I believe Kyra is headed in that direction as well. I'm off to see if I may be of service."

"Nay - you will not. Your uncle would have my head if he thought I humored you thusly. You won't go any further than the middle wall - do you *ken*? It is night fall and near past your curfew."

"Aye – I hear you Odhran," grumbled Darina. "I must see Lucian though, to determine how Riann got loose this time. I can't seem to secure her of late. She is always about when she should be in her quarters on her perch."

"Nay, my lady. Lucian is long past slumbering and Riann is returning even now. You can speak with her yourself," he chuckled under his breath. "Perhaps she should reside in your room with you if you wish to keep a better eye on her."

Darina could not contain the look of disdain and rebellion that rose up over her neck and sent a deep flush over her face. *Always being told what to do. I am so tired of being treated as a child. Soon – I shall be married and no one will have such control over me, I will be the Laird's wife and I will be in control for once.*

"Not bloody likely."

"Dervilla, you liked to have scared the skin off of me," Darina retorted. "What on earth are you doing up at this hour?"

"I came to see what has become of your precious Riann. I went in to give her some mice, and she was missing again from her perch. When I heard her cries, I assumed she had gone out with Kyra to intercept the rider."

"Can I have no thoughts that are mine alone, dear sister?"

134

"I'm not sure, can you?" retorted Dervilla. "You've never been good at hiding your feelings Darina; it isn't very hard at all to surmise your thoughts."

"For once, let's not pretend you don't know what I'm talking about - now can't we? We both know how you enjoy trespassing in areas you don't belong Dervilla. I've long suspected that Lucian has had quite a bit to do with it as well."

"Oh Lucian, but how you enjoy blaming him for so many things, Darina. He told mother you have the gift as well."

Bloody hell he did. What vivid imaginations those two conjured together. The "gifts," the "curses," the "blessings", the nonsense! All of it - pagan nonsense!

"Darina, one day you will wish you had paid more attention to this nonsense."

"I think not. You with all your gods and shamans have never succeeded in breaking any curses you believe hover over our land, placed there - may I add - by other pagans!"

Nay - I've no use for any of it. God, god, gods, goddesses - NONSENSE!

"I seem to recall, Darina, a time when Father MacArtrey had nearly convinced you to take the vows of an Anchoress."

"And - what of it?"

"You didn't seem to think it such nonsense then."

"Well, that was many years ago. I grew tired of Lucian's teachings. None of his stories ever made sense to me. I was looking for something that would make sense, not just another shaman."

"Lucian is not just another shaman and you know it, Darina. He is the last in a long line of O'Malley clan holy men. And he is doing his best to make sure that all the rites, ceremonies, and knowledge are passed down for future generations."

"Dervilla, believe what you will. Worship as many gods or goddesses or things as you like - just leave me be. And - stay out of my head!"

"Darina, I fear for you. Your gifts are as strong as or stronger than mothers were. Yet, you deny them."

"I have no gifts, save my intellect. I refuse to use whatever intellect I may have to interfere with other people's lives. It's manipulative and it's wrong."

SIXTEEN

O'Malley Lands

Damn, my backside still aches. I shall never get used to this new saddle. Kyra's horse cleared the last of the small bridges that encased the moats outside the castle walls and made her way around the winding path up towards the clearing. The rider in the distance grew closer and she could clearly see the outline of Riann sitting atop the rider's left shoulder.

Father. Thank the gods.

"Father!" she yelled as she waived her O'Malley clan flag which sat atop her spear. "Welcome home."

Riann left her perch on Ruarc's shoulder and took back to the skies, flying so high above head that it appeared she topped the setting sun, before turning and plunging to earth at break neck speed. When Riann swooped back up, it appeared she had a rabbit or small rodent in her claws. *All in day's work, my love.*

Ruarc's steed grew restless and increased his pace towards the grounds meeting Kyra before she had guessed he would.

"So father, how was the journey?" she asked.

"Fine indeed," he replied. "Except for the few days we were on MacCahan land, it stormed the entire time we were there - even after you left. They are in dire need of our assistance in rebuilding much of their village."

"I've never seen the likes of it," replied Kyra. "Never - such weather indeed. It has been most pleasant here, it grows a little colder by the day, but otherwise, it has been smooth and sunny. Should make for a fine wedding I believe."

"Aye - a wedding," said Ruarc. "Won't this be a most interesting year, Kyra?"

"A bit of advice father - if you will?"

"Go ahead then Kyra, what have you to say?"

"You would do well to head straight to the inn, else Darina realize it's you and keep you up all night with her interrogations."

A deep chuckle escaped Ruarc's throat and threatened to spill humorous tears behind his gray eyes. "Kyra - how you do make me laugh."

"I've no need to avoid Darina; I have nothing to offer her by way of information anyhow."

"Alright - but don't say I didn't try to warn you father."

＊

Patrick paced before the fire fully aware of the faces studying his and how the implications of his dreams might play out. Speaking slowly, he managed to finish his tale quicker than he thought and sat down to enjoy his ale.

"Well - I see nothing out of the ordinary about that. 'Tis no omen, Carbry", directed Deasum. "Just a dream, it could have been the rabbit stew," he chuckled.

"I doubt th-that," replied Patrick, clearly not amused.

"Why is that?" asked Carbry.

"Because of the strange lass," interrupted Braeden. "Tell them about the strange lass, Patrick, tell them. He's seen her in his dreams before."

Mavis spoke, "Patrick is there something more you haven't told us?"

"No-not really."

"Not really?" asked Deasum.

"Go ahead, Patrick, tell them," said Braeden.

"Well I am s-su-sure my dream means nothing."

"And just how are you sure, Patrick?" asked Carbry.

"Because w-wh-what I saw could not be real. That is to s-s-say, it would not be t-tru-true, it would be but a d-de-delusion."

"How is that you say?" inquired Deasum.

"Because of the strange lass in the dream," said Braeden.

"How is the lass strange?" asked Mavis. "What does she look like?"

"She looks l-like a n-nor-normal lass. She has long red hair, pretty gr-green eyes - a bonnie l-lass indeed."

"Then if she looks normal what is strange about her?" demanded Deasum.

"'Tis what she wore," said Braeden matter-of-factly.

"What she wore?" demanded Carbry as he rose to face Patrick on the other side of the camp fire. "What did she wear Patrick? Tell us!"

"She wore truis".

SEVENTEEN

Burke Lands - Odetta's Monastery

"Has he finally sobered yet?" asked Odetta to Easal.

"Enough I believe - but it took a lot of doing and most of the healer's kudzu vine to get him there."

Odetta stood beside Easal looking over the soaking wet body of Father MacArtrey that lay in a crumpled manner over the bench just outside the monastery garden.

"And what of this?" she inquired. Easal shrugged his shoulders, "He stank too much, and the healer refused us help lest we bathe him."

"And his clothes? I realize it's been raining, but he is soaked through and his boots as well."

"They stank as well my lady."

Odetta let out a cackling laugh that Easal was sure would wake the devil.

"What shall I do with him?"

"Wake him and take him to the altar. He will perform the rites tonight. Call for Naelyn and have her bring the others as well.

The sun had almost completely set and the only light to be seen came from the twin torches which were perched on either side of the altar hearth in the monastery. Odetta had the benches brought in and closed the tapestries over the windows so that the rain would not interfere with their task.

"Set to lighting the candles," she instructed several young girls who sat in the back of the sanctum. "And move that chest to just below the window, stoke the fire - and Naelyn," she interjected, "Don't forget the cistern and holy water."

"Yes, my lady," replied Naelyn. "Shall you have need of the sacred dagger?"

"Aye, yes indeed. Bring the dagger of Teutates; it is necessary for the ceremony. Bring someone to wipe his sniveling face," shouted Odetta as she motioned towards the young boy still tied to the altar pedestal.

The chamber quickly became full, bustling with activity in preparation for the great service. Tonight they would give thanks to Teutates, their god of war, fertility and wealth for the abundance they had been blessed with over the prior year; and they would pray - for war.

***

"Hold still now! I've only a few more stitches and we will be done and you can get back to your precious bird Darina," grunted Darina's younger sister Darcy. "I'm almost done, and it looks magnificent if I do say so myself."

"I would have to agree," quipped Kyra from the other side of the chamber. "Her bird is precious to her." Kyra laughed clearly attempting to rile Darina's temper.

"She's not a bird you nitwits, she is a Peregrine Falcon and she has more royalty in her lineage than all of us put together. "She is a fine falcon, fit for a prince."

"But - stuck with a shrew! Aye Darcy?" Kyra and Darcy burst into contagious laughter that seemed lost on Darina.

"I realize the both of you are having fun at my expense, but neither of you seem to understand the true gravity of my situation."

"Your situation, my dear sister?" inquired Darcy.

"Yes, her situation," interjected Kyra. "Let me see if I can explain it."

"Oh please do so, by all means Kyra," retorted Darina as she rolled her eyes.

"Well, if I am to understand correctly; Darina is to be married in two evenings. Patrick MacCahan is his name. He is one of the handsomest men in all of Ireland. He comes from a well-respected family, he is tall, strong, fit and healthy, trained as a warrior, and he has agreed to leave his home to make this union with a woman he has never met, to protect a clan he does not know, and to establish a shipping enterprise with the territories in Northern Ireland to further aid the prosperity we have so richly been blessed with here in O'Malley territory. Does that about sum it up, Darina?"

"You have the right of it, Kyra. It just sounds differently when you put it that way."

"Oh wait, I forgot the best part."

"Which is that?" asked Darcy.

"Darina actually gets to be married - which is more than I can say for either of us. There are no men to be had here, and I don't see there being any other noble characters out there just waiting to leave their homes to join with us. All we will have to look forward to, Darcy, is the Bacchanal festivals."

"Bring in the looking glass Odhran, Darina must see this," yelled Darcy.

"I'll do it," said Ruarc gruffly from the threshold of her chamber door. "You look divine Darina, a picture of a lady, just like your dear mother."

"I'm so sorry you couldn't wear mother's dress Darina, you are simply too tall, you have a good four inches on her. But I made the best replica I could."

"Here - turn and see," directed Kyra.

Instantly, Darina was mesmerized by the image in the looking glass. She did indeed favor her mother and the dress was near to exact as her mother's - save a few custom details that Darcy had added.

The ivory dress was covered with golden stitching throughout, it tightly hugged her form and draped to the floor, flowing as if it were a river. The long sleeves which ended right at the curve of her wrist gave it an ethereal feel. The sharp pointed bodice was overlaid with pearl on the lace edging and joined the skirt which hung ankle length. The O'Malley red and blue plaid was fastened about her waist and hung in ripples about her hips. Her younger sister had woven gold, silver and sapphire colored cross stitch patterns around the hem which was longer in the back to create a train. A red dragon adorned each sleeve – the symbol of the O'Malley Clan. It had a semi overcoat of luscious see through red and blue silk which tied at her back after draping across her shoulders.

"It's perfect," noted Darcy. "Simply perfect."

"I love it," replied Darina.

"It seems to be missing something," offered Ruarc scratching his beard in contemplation.

"But what?" questioned Kyra.

"Aye – I know what it is." Ruarc stepped forward and handed Darina a small velvet pouch.

"What is this?" she questioned.

"It is a gift from your betrothed. He bade me to present it to you when I arrived."

Darina held the pouch in awe at its beauty, hesitant to open it for fear of breaking something.

"Go ahead Darina, see what it is," implored Darcy.

147

Darina sat at the edge of her bed and pondered the contents of the velvet pouch. Carefully she untied the package and peeked inside.

"It is beautiful," she said.

"Well — let me see it," cried Kyra. "Come on now, hand it over. We haven't got all day."

Darina rose from the bed and held out the jeweled hair comb embedded with sapphires and rubies, with its flowing ribbons for all to see.

"Why it's a perfect match," announced Darcy. "Wherever did he find something of this value?"

"He must have spent a fortune on that," added Kyra.

"Nay," said Ruarc. "It's of more value than you know."

"What do you mean," asked Darina.

"It was his mother's comb; she wore it on her wedding day, a gift from her father."

Darina paced the room, a troubled look on her face. *His mother's? I have no idea who this man is, let alone his mother. What fate awaits me?*

"My - aren't you a picture, dear sister?" asked Dervilla from the door.

"A picture of what, that is the question, isn't it cousin?" quipped Kyra under her breath.

"Now, now girls let's be civil," said Ruarc. "Darina has a destiny to fulfill in a few short days' time and she seems troubled."

"Darina - what troubles you lass?"

"I'm not sure, I have a feeling something is not quite right. I can't put my finger on it, but I'm sure; something is amiss."

"Darina, you denied your gifts years ago. Why pretend now?" asked Dervilla.

"It is not a pretense Dervilla; I can feel it - evil in our midst."

"Ruarc, what manner of man is Patrick MacCahan?" asked Darina.

"A fine man Darina, you needn't worry, he is the most noble of gentleman."

"And - when will they arrive?"

"By tomorrow eve, I suspect. You shall be joined in two night's time."

"I see. Leave me. All of you."

"I must remove the dress sister," said Darcy. "I will help you get undressed and then I will leave."

"Shall I send to the kitchens for your supper?" asked Kyra.

"Nay - I am not feeling hungry. I do feel that I may …"

Oh no. I do not wish to faint, my stomach, my head. I am so dizzy. Darina clutched her stomach and bent over sure she would vomit right there.

"Oh - no you don't," said Darcy as she grabbed the chamber pot and placed it under Darina. "In the pot my dear - and don't you dare get it on my dress."

"Your dress?" inquired Darina. "I know what you mean," said Darina now on her knees clutching the side of the bed.

"It's just wedding jitters Darina, nothing more," chuckled Ruarc. "You'll be fine; most brides get a bit anxious before they are joined. In a few days' time, you will be right as rain."

"I am not so confident of that," said Dervila. "Look at her she - is four shades green."

"Leave me!" Darina commanded.

"Nay!" exclaimed Minea as she entered the chamber. "She is not having jitters, she is sick. Looks to me like she has been poisoned."

"Poison?" asked Ruarc.

"Yes, Poison."

"Now - send for Atilde, I have need of her healing services," said Minea.

"Nay. I will get Lucian, he will fix this," said Dervilla.

EIGHTEEN

Burke Lands - Odetta's Monastery

The chanting subsided as the sound of rain hitting the roof lulled the group into silence. Odetta unchained the boy and presented him to the group.

"Our sacrifice!" Odetta shouted as a large cloud of black smoke erupted from the hearth. "Teutates is most pleased."

Odetta motioned for Father MacArtrey and Easal to join her near the altar. Naelyn brought a carafe of holy water forward and motioned for the priest to fill each follower's glass with a portion of it.

"Odetta, you know I cannot be a part of this witchcraft," he said. "It is forbidden, I risk my very soul."

"I've no use for your soul, Father – and you will do as you are told, else you become the sacrifice."

The boy shouted, "No," through his tears and tugged vehemently at the ropes now held by Easal - to no avail. "Please let me go, my father will pay handsomely for my ransom. I assure you."

"Dear boy, I've no need of money. I have everything I want, and soon, your blood will ensure my dominion over this land and all of its inhabitants."

"Father, you know what to do, now do it."

A look of terror overtook Father MacArtrey as he strode closer to the boy. "Please forgive me son," he whispered. "Child, this will all be over soon, you will see. And it won't hurt ever much, I promise. Just do what I tell you."

"Don't comfort the bastard you insolent priest. Get on with it."

"Very well."

Cynbel arose from the shadows and handed Father MacArtrey the dagger of Teutates. He unsheathed the magnificent blade and turned to address the congregation.

"*By the moon, the stars and the skies;*
we offer this sacrifice to Teutates.

His chosen ones this day unite,
to partake o'the innocent one's -
life force within the blood.
Our sacrifice this day be for
the ancient rite of holy war!"

At the sound of the war rite, the gatherers shouted, "War, war, war, war, war!" in unified voice. They began to chant, wail and moan and the musty odor of peat fire filled the altar.

"Now," commanded Odetta.

"Very well," replied Father MacArtrey and grabbed the boy by the left hand. "By Teutates, I accept your sacrifice" and he sliced a long line upon the boy's left wrist. "Naelyn quickly," he murmured, "the cisterns."

Naelyn grabbed the sacred cisterns and placed them beneath the bleeding arm of the boy who was screaming and near to passing out. His blood trickled a line of red all around the altar and began filling the cisterns. When he had finally passed out, Father MacArtrey laid him to the side of the altar and covered him with his cloak.

"Come my people and drink in the rite!" exclaimed Odetta, as each gatherer brought their glass of holy water to mix it with the blood of the boy's sacrifice.

"Drink your fill, this night we celebrate!"

"To war," she exclaimed as she raised her glass.

"To war," came the loud replies. "To war!"

* * *

"Mary, Mother of God," said Deasum under his breath and began to pace back and forth in front of the fire.

"Mavis, begin packing, we leave at once," instructed Carbry.

"But my lords," interrupted Mavis.

"Mavis, please do as you are asked, and at once." shouted Deasum sternly. "I mean to leave post haste."

Patrick rose from the log where he was sitting and placed a hand on Deasum's shoulder. "Deasum, what on earth is b-both-bothering you man? It is n-ne-near to sunrise and you wish to traverse Burke lands in the d-da-day light?"

"We must, we've no other choice. Darina's safety depends on it."

"Darina's safety depends on us ignoring our safety and traveling through Burke lands in the day?" inquired Mavis. "I

155

will not go, I will stay here or turn back; I will not go in the daylight."

"Mavis, hold on a bit," commanded Patrick.

"Deasum, I must kn-know what is going on. Why must we l-leave now."

"I can't explain it to you," replied Deasum.

"You can and you w-wi-will. I am to be the new l-la-laird in two days' time. You wil t-tell me n-now, or you will t-tell me then. Either way, I w-won't budge an inch lest you tell me."

"Very well - It's the girl, the girl in your dreams."
"What of her?"

"She is Darina, your betrothed."

"Wh-what? How do you know?"

"It is she, I am certain of it."

"Tell me how!"

"Patrick, she wears, she wears men's - she wears truis and she is our clan falconer," retorted Deasum shaking his head in anguish and rubbing his eyes with his fists.

"Falconer?"

"Yes, her falcon's name is Riann. She is the best in Western Ireland. The dream you had, it is a foretelling, Darina is in danger, and we must get to her at once."

"I see."

"Mavis," Patrick directed to Braeden's nurse. "I canna protect you if you remain behind. We are already on the b-border of B-Burke lands. But I willna force you to c-come with us. Braeden n-needs you, I would be mo-most appreciative if you w-wou-would join us on the road."

"Very well, my lord," she replied. "But I wish to ride in the back of the carts under the coverings.

"As you w-wi-wish."

NINETEEN

O'Malley Castle

"Darina, can you hear me my love? Darina please answer me, can you hear me?" came the worn inquisition from Minea.

There must be a horse sitting atop my head. I just know it. And why won't they please hold their tongues? It pains me so.

"She has lain in this bed for nigh on three nights now. Not a word, not a moan even," said Minea.

Who are they talking about and why won't they just be quiet?

"And – you're sure it was poison?" asked Ruarc from his perch standing at the arrow slit window watching the sun fade in the distance.

"Quite sure," stated Lucian. "I have every confidence though that she will make a full recovery. The herbs and elixirs prepared by myself and Atilde have done their job. It is only to wait now - only to wait."

"Kyra - any word from the priest?" questioned Ruarc as he turned to face the group gathered around Darina's bed.

"Nothing father," she responded. "When I and Murchadh searched for him we discovered his chambers empty and the chapel unkempt. It appeared he left in a hurry. In fact, we aren't totally sure he left willingly but we haven't sent a search party for him as of yet. Murchadh believes it best we leave our troops intact until the others arrive."

"Aye, Murchadh is one of the wisest of my men, I trust his judgment. What bothers me daughter is that the wedding was to have taken place two nights ago, and Father MacArtrey, I do not believe, would have left the honors to anyone else. I do believe he would have been here and knew we expected him to be."

"I think you insulted him however, Ruarc, when you suggested the wedding not take place in the chapel. When we set to make the plans, Lucian mentioned the overlook cliff above the bay, he seemed quite perturbed," interrupted Atilde.

Ruarc chastised her with his eyes and continued, "However, I do wish to send a few men out to receive the travelers, they should have been here by now and I feel a storm is brewing, it's best we do this now, Kyra."

"As you wish father, may I accompany?" asked Kyra.

"As you wish, Kyra." he replied.

"Lucian, would you send Riann out ahead of the group, to lead the way? I fear we need another set of eyes on the road."

Nay. Do not send Riann, she may get lost or hurt, or a hunter may take her. She should not go out without me. Do you hear me, are you listening?

"Father - she is trying to tell us something." exclaimed Kyra.

"Quick - get her some water," uttered Lucian.

Darina blinked behind heavy eyelids and licked her swollen, cracked lips. *So thirsty, and hungry! How long have I been here?*

"What is going on?" she asked.

"Darina! By the gods! We thought we had lost you!" exclaimed Atilde. "Don't try to move too fast, you have been awfully sick. You were poisoned."

"Poisoned! By whom? Who would want to harm me?"

"Now wait a minute dear, take your time sitting up, unless you want to retch some more."

"Not bloody likely, I think I could eat a goat and I dare say there is nothing left in my belly," she said.

Darina opened her eyes fully and began to search the faces of those in the room. It grew dark, but the fire was lit to a blaze and the candles on either side of her bed shown bright. She carefully peered over the countenance of all who gathered around her and broke an inquisitive gaze.

"Well, where is he? Where has he gone?"

"Who my dear?" asked Lucian.

"The monk of course – he was there, in the corner. *Although I'm not quite sure if he is a monk or a priest - to be honest.*

"Well? Where did he go?"

"Of whom do you speak, Darina?" questioned Lucian again.

"The monk, he stood right there in the corner," she said pointing to the far side of the hearth. "And he spoke to me the entire time I've been confined to this bed. He said prayers, he chanted, he held my hand, he comforted me. He even fed me in the wee hours of the night when no one else was in my room. Where did he go?"

Lucian gave Ruarc a skeptical look and rose to sit next to Darina on the bed. He placed her feeble hand inside his and caressed her palm with his thumb.

"Darina, tell me - what does this monk look like?"

"A monk - for heaven's sake! He wore black robes and a cloak and had a golden rope tied about his waist. Just like a monk!"

"Describe his features Darina, so I can be sure of whom you speak."

"Very well then. He was tall, possibly the tallest man I ever did see," she chuckled.

"Why do you giggle," asked Kyra.

"I could just see Darcy trying to get material enough to clothe the man," Darina stated through her giggles.

"She is delirious with fever," Ruarc interjected.

"No I'm not, I have no fever and I know what or rather whom, I saw. Now - tell me who he is."

Lucian continued, "Go on my dear, what else? He was tall, and….?"

"Oh he had long, brownish red wavy hair that hung past his shoulders and green eyes, the color of spring grass. He was a rather large man to be a monk I would say, but what do I know?"

"My, my, my," said Lucian as he rose to pace the room.

"Well – where did he go?" demanded Darina.

"Darina, Ruarc and I shall get to the bottom of this quickly, for now, eat your supper and regain your strength; we shall talk in the morning."

"Wait a minute," commanded Darina. "Do not take Riann with you please. I couldn't bear it if something were to happen to her."

"Dear child, I would never let anything happen to Riann, you know this." he replied. "Now get your rest."

★★★

Lightening pierced the sky and chased the thunder clap. The rain was like needles upon their skin, and yet Deasum bade they continue. The rocky terrain was hazardous and Patrick had changed the last wheel his father had sent when Deasum halted them for a rest and to partake of a brief meal.

"Patrick, might I wander on a bit behind the trees?" asked Braeden. "I need to relieve myself."

"I pr-pref-prefer you wait until I or Ca-Carbry may accompany you."

"But I have to go bad! Besides it is well past sunset, we made good ground today during the daylight and haven't seen hide or hair of any Burke clansman."

Deasum interjected, "I see no harm in it, and we are getting close to the border that separates Burke lands from O'Malley lands. I dare say we may make it just after sunrise if we don't rest too long."

"I'll see to him," said Mavis. "I have need of a little wandering myself."

"Don't g-go far," warned Patrick.

"We will see you in a bit then," called Mavis over her shoulder.

They walked west towards the bustling stream they had crossed miles back, knowing it probably flowed in their direction. The rain itself wasn't too much of a burden, but the wind whipped the tree limbs about them and made their journey slow. Thunder serenaded them and lightening lit their way until finally they came upon a small patch of thick brush just this side of the stream.

"We will stop here," Mavis said and pointed Braeden towards the brush. "Go on now, be about your business."

***

"Patrick, have you had any other dreams to speak of?" inquired Carbry.

"Nay - n-no-not really."

"Not really?" questioned Deasum a concerned look upon his face.

"No. None."

Carbry shot Deasum a concerned glanced and rose to question Patrick further when he heard an almost inhuman scream in the distance.

"Mavis," they said in unison.

TWENTY

Burke Lands - Odetta's Monastery

When the last of the cups were empty, Odetta rose to speak. "My people - we have great promise. Our sacrifice to Teutates is welcomed and we are assured our war!"

Cheers rose up in the hall and Easal bent his knee to Odetta in reverence. The entire hall followed his lead, save for Father MacArtrey and Cynbel.

"My dear priest, I understand your reluctance to bow your knee, but you will soon enough. Of that I am most certain. It is you my dear brother that surprises me so."

Odetta turned and stepped down from the platform to face her brother.

"And why would the Laird of this clan bow his knee to a mere woman?" asked Cynbel Burke.

"A mere woman, you say?" inquired Odetta.

"A mere woman, indeed."

"Can a mere woman call upon the gods to do her bidding? Can a mere woman wield the power to make war?"

"You can't make war without warriors, sister. Surely you aren't as deft as you look?" replied Cynbel. "No Burke soldiers will march upon your orders, and you know this."

"But of course; but they *will* march upon the orders of my husband - will they not?" she asked as she gestured towards Easal.

Easal rose acknowledging her inference and paced to stand beside her in front of Cynbel.

"And why would your marriage - to anyone - have any bearing whatsoever upon the loyalty of *my* soldiers?"

"It would if you were dead."

Odetta unsheathed the dagger of Teutates and thrust it madly into her brother Cynbel's chest. Cynbel staggered and tilted forward before gripping Easal by his hips and pleading with him with his eyes.

"Easal, why have you betrayed me?" he asked, before he sputtered blood from his mouth and collapsed on the floor beside Father MacArtrey.

Father MacArtrey quickly took a knee before Odetta could utter another word.

"Well that didn't take as long as I originally thought," she said as she rose and retook her position before the group at the altar.

"This day I shall marry Easal, who will become your new Laird. "You shall all, each of you, pledge your allegiance to our union and this war we are to undertake by blood oath!"

"Blood oath?" inquired the priest.

"Yes," whispered Naelyn in his ear. "We shall each of us cut the palm of our right hands and drip our blood into the cistern. When we have all done it, Odetta and Easal will partake of our offering and they shall gain great power with the gods."

"Wickedness," replied the priest.

"The greatest form," replied Naelyn, smiling eerily.

***

Breacan MacCahan rose from table and trudged towards his youngest son Payton who slumped glibly across the bench in front of the hearth.

"I ask you to do this for your brother, Payton. He needs you and you know I cannot send Parkin at this time, when we are beginning construction on the piers. It must be you and you will take fifty or so of our strongest unmarried men with you."

"Father, explain to me one more time, what I am needed *for*," said Payton, reluctantly.

"It is not for you to question me son; it is for you to simply do my will."

"Why the need for the men, father?"

"To protect your brother and his new clan."

"To protect them from what, father?"

"Why must you ask so many questions, Payton? You try my patience." Breacan hovered above his son, an angry scowl upon his face.

"Now rise, prepare for your journey and I will send word that you are on your way."

"How long am I to remain at my brother's service?"

"Until he says otherwise!"

"And will that message come on the wings of a falcon?" asked Payton snidely.

"What do you know of a falcon?" asked the Laird, heat rising in his face.

"I know that I have seen such a falcon, that it often rests outside your balcony overlooking the battlements. I know that I've seen you bring it inside and that later, you send it outside and it flies away. I've seen this happen many times over the years, father. And — I assume it is the same falcon, although I cannot surmise how it happens to remain alive after all this time."

"Payton — I warn you. Say nothing of this falcon to anyone. Do you understand me?"

"Aye father. I will say nothing to no one, if you tell me what is going on."

"Payton, this falcon is a messenger sent from the O'Malley clan. There is threat of war upon their clan and I am sending you to assist your brother. That is all."

"I think not, father. I have heard rumor there is magic involved here and I've no doubt that the O'Malley's do not know the full truth of my brother's identity."

Breacan grabbed his youngest son Payton by the nape of the neck and forced him to rise from the bench. His hands shook with anger and fear and he struggled for words.

"Payton, you will do nothing and say nothing at this time that may cause your brother or the O'Malleys any harm. Your curiosity will get the better of you and you may find your own life in danger if you cannot control yourself."

Sweat rose on Payton's brow and he grew limp in surrender to his father's grasp. He raised both palms and held them out in a display of submission and his father let him loose.

"Now - enemies we have - all of us. Do not make an enemy of me, my son."

TWENTY - ONE

Burke Lands - Odetta's Monastery

"Why Father MacArtrey, you look quite peeked and pale. Tell me, have you never seen a man killed?" inquired Odetta.

"I have witnessed the travesties of war. I am familiar with bloodshed. I have never seen it done to a beloved family member, if that is what you mean," the priest replied.

"Beloved family member, indeed," Odetta cackled. Easal erupted in laughter and Naelyn stood before him with the dagger awaiting his palm.

"Father, it is time," whispered Naelyn. "Let me have your hand. You are the last."

The priest reluctantly walked forward towards the altar and the waiting cistern. Before she could roll his sleeve to clench his hand, Naelyn gasped.

"You - you already bleed!" she shrieked.

"What?" cried Odetta. "Let me see."

Odetta reached towards him, grabbed the priest's arm and raised his sleeve. Blood dripped from his right hand and he swayed as if he were about to faint.

"What have you done?" shouted Easal.

"Throw him in the dungeons!" commanded Odetta. "And find that boy!" With that, Father MacArtrey dropped to the floor of the chamber, trickling blood pooling around him.

"What do you mean, my lady? What has happened?" inquired Naelyn.

"Can't you see, he added his own blood to the cisterns, the ceremony - is invalid. We have no promise of victory at war."

"What?"

"Think you nit-wit! He spared the boy, by adding his own blood to the cisterns. We sent to have the boy's body disposed of but no doubt the boy still lives!"

"But - I saw the wound on the child."

"Of course you did. No doubt he cut him, he just wasn't drained fully."

"Oh, no."

"What will become of the priest?"

"For now, he can rot below with the others."

"Wait!" exclaimed Naelyn.

"Whatever for?" asked Odetta. "Don't tell me you harbor a soft spot for the priest."

"No, my lady. But if he should perish below we may never find the whereabouts of the missing scrolls."

Odetta turned towards Easal and summoned her manservant, Gial. "She's right of course, put him in a guest chamber and send for the healer, we will speak with him when he revives. We must have the scrolls."

★★★

The stench of filthy linens, stale beer and rotten wood permeated the air as Kyra and Murchadh entered the chambers of Father MacArtrey. His chamber was nestled inside a small round house with a thatched roof that sat behind the chapel. The door was wide open and the dirt floor was damp from the light rain which had fallen that morning.

"I've no idea where he's gone, but he has no doubt been missing for some time, by the looks of things," said Murchadh.

174

"Aye. Not much of a neat keep is he?" she replied.

Murchadh continued, "By the looks of it, I'd say he left in quite a bit of a hurry. Look – the table is over turned, the fire has burned out and it appears there may have been a struggle. I think those are foot prints – it's just hard to tell with the rain blowing in."

"It appears he hasn't lost his taste for the spirits," commented Kyra as she held up one of many bottles of ale that lay strewn across the floor.

"No doubt of that."

"I spoke with Moya, his horse remains at the stables. And look – his robes still hang on the peg."

"Something is amiss here, Kyra."

"I agree, but now we must go to intercept Deasum and Carbry. I'm not sure what can be done about the priest – we have more pressing concerns," she replied.

"I'll fix the table and straighten the mess if you will see to the door. Make sure it can be secured."

"Aye," was his short reply.

A man of few words. I like that about you Murchadh. Now, Father MacArtrey 'tis not my concern the condition of your chambers. However, I will secure your belongings in your

absence.

Kyra straightened the table and set the stool upright as she gathered the mugs and bottles of ale together in a pile for waste. When she was done she stood and wiped her hands on her truis and turned towards Murchadh.

"Shall we go?"

"Not yet, let's burn those bed covers. They reek," he said.

"I agree."

Together they turned to remove the linens from the straw mattress that sat upon the wooden platform bed frame. When they made to turn the bed, their eyes locked in astonishment.

"A false top — there's a hidden chamber!" she cried.

"Open it."

Kyra carefully removed the disguised top piece centered in the middle of the platform frame. Inside sat a small chest embellished with jewels and scrolls that looked to be very old.

"Open the chest."

Inside the chest, Kyra found coin, jewels and deeds to lands. "The chapel funds."

"Aye," Murchadh nodded.

"What do you make of these scrolls?"

"I've no idea."

TWENTY - TWO

The border between O'Malley Lands and Burke Lands

Deasum, Carbry and Patrick all donned their armor belts and swords and shot through the forest like cannon balls seeking their aim. The screaming grew louder as the men struggled through the heavy rains to locate the commotion.

"Mavis! Mavis!" they yelled through the driving rain and sound of thunder.

"I see something," shouted Carbry, leading the way.

Almost twenty yards into the trees, the boy stood still in the moonlight, grasping a tree and drenching from rain - his face stained with mud and blood.

"Dear God - it's Bra-Braeden," said Patrick as he knelt beside the boy who had now collapsed to his knees in shock. His teeth chattered involuntarily and he looked ahead into the distance, almost unaware of his surroundings.

Patrick shook him. "Br-Braeden - where is M-Mavis?"

Silence.

"Braeden - where is M-mavis?"

Nothing.

"Deasum, g-goo on ahead. Carbry, stay h-he-ere with Braeden. No - take him b-ba-ack to c-ca-amp and guard him. D-de-easum, I'm right behind you."

Mavis' screams grew louder as they closed the distance to the stream. The echo of marching water mixed with the thunder and rain made it nearly impossible to discern what was happening. When they stepped outside of the clearing to stand near the water's edge, they saw her.

In the firm grip of a soldier, Mavis stood looking at something that lay on the ground. Deasum motioned for Patrick to move off to the left, nearly behind where the man stood holding Mavis with his dagger to her neck. Deasum moved forward until Mavis spotted him. He raised one finger to his mouth in search of her silence and he was successful.

Deasum raised his sword with his right hand and walked into clear sight of the soldier. Mavis struggled against the man who tightened his grip on her right arm. A small trickle of blood rain down her collar bone.

"Leave her be," commanded Deasum as he took small steps towards the man, closing the gap between them. "Release her!" he shouted as he pulled a small axe from behind his back and held it in his left hand.

"This will not end well for you," he continued. "Let her be."

Mavis locked eyes with Deasum and gestured with them to her feet, just in front of her as if trying to communicate. Deasum began to stalk his opponent, first left then right he moved; forcing his opponent away from the water's edge in hope's that Patrick could attempt a sneak attack.

When the man had finally turned them to face completely away from the stream, Patrick spoke, "L-live or die, my friend. Live or d-di-ie. Your ch-choice." The man jumped in surprise and Mavis kicked behind her until her foot met his knee cap and he struggled forward, releasing the blade he held at her throat.

"Your ch-choice," repeated Patrick as Deasum circled behind him. In a futile act of defiance the soldier turned and raised his sword towards Deasum as Patrick lunged from behind; one swift swing of his blade and the soldier stood there for mere seconds - headless - until his body crumpled to the muddy ground.

Deasum turned to find Mavis with her back to him on the ground grasping her neck with her left hand and holding something in her lap with her right. On the ground, in the mud and rain, lay a young boy covered in blood and wrapped in a meager looking cloak. His hair had been freshly shaven and his wrist was slashed open. It had been crudely wrapped in linen cloth and tied off.

Patrick walked towards them to survey the damage to Mavis before realizing what she held. "Dear God, wh-what is this?" he asked.

Mavis ventured to speak before Deasum bade her silent. "We must get you - both of you - out of this rain and tend to your wounds."

"I'll carry the boy if you will see to Mavis," he directed to Patrick.

***

"It's nice to see you up and about sister," said Dervilla as Darina headed down the front stairs towards the kitchens. "We broke our fast several hours ago, but I'm sure you will find some pastries left over if you like."

Darina walked towards the high table and hearth and sat down on a bench beside her sister who was working on a set of maps she had spread open.

"What are you working on Dervilla?" she asked.

"I'm updating the charts on our border with the Burke clan. Lucian asked me to ensure it was updated, and to make a rudimentary drawing for Kyra and Murchadh to take with them. There are a few places where the streams have diverted or dried up altogether since they were last updated."

"Where exactly are they heading?"

"To intercept Deasum and the group traveling from MacCahan lands. They should have been here already. Our uncle Ruarc grows concerned that they haven't. Although, a few merchants have indicated the weather has been testy, it seems it's been storming somewhat near the border."

"I see. Then I shall have no reprieve?" asked Darina.

"I think not sister. You will most certainly be married shortly," she chuckled.

"Has Father MacArtrey returned?"

"Nay - he hasn't. I believe the next order of business will be to find him. If he does not return soon, Lucian shall perform the ceremony."

Darina rose and paced before the great hearth. She surveyed the room with sentimentality. Portraits of her parents and her grandparents adorned the walls - commissioned by her father prior to his death. Woven tapestries depicting victory at war hung above the entry walls, and the stone floors were dressed in elaborate rugs from India.

"Dervilla, Lucian is a druid," she said.

"Yes. What of it?" asked Dervilla.

"I am not a druid."

"Does it matter? Lucian worships the old gods, Father MacArtrey the new god and you worship no god. I see no problem," Dervilla replied.

"In two nights it will be Samhain, the new year. Do you suspect Ruarc will wish to see me wed on Samhain and by a druid priest?" asked Darina.

"It is possible, especially if Father MacArtrey is not located before your betrothed arrives."

"Dervilla - I am not lacking in spiritual matters."

"I didn't say you were."

"But you imply I worship no god."

"Whom do you worship Darina?"

"No one. Myself. I rely upon myself and nothing else. No Pagan god or Christian god has altered my life. However, a pagan priestess has plagued our clan for over twenty years. I can't say that her druid roots give me much hope for their cause."

"You can't compare all druids to Odetta Burke, sister. She is not a true druid, she is a woman who has tapped into magic and uses it for her own personal agenda. Lucian is not that way."

"Aye. I know. It still leaves me suspect of all religions. No good has come from any of them. Prove me wrong."

"I've no need sister," replied Dervilla.

"And why is that?"

"Darina, follow your heart. That's all I will tell you. You know what it is you need and others know what it is they need. The best we can do is to live just and honorable lives and cause harm to none."

"Harm to none? What of those who cause harm to us?"

"That is the question sister, is it not?"

TWENTY - THREE

Burke Lands

"My lady, he is awake," said Naelyn as she entered Odetta's chambers.

Odetta pushed the linens back and arose from the bed stark naked, spent from her dalliance with Easal, her new husband. She grabbed her cloak and pulled her black hair back into a braid that fell just below her shoulder blades.

"See that he is not disturbed," she said and pointed to Easal who lay snoring contentedly. "And have some food brought in a bit - set it on the table in the corner."

"Yes, my lady. Shall we go?" asked Naelyn.

"Aye. We shall."

The air was thick in the make shift chamber which had been prepared for the priest. Used previously as a storage room, there was little light and only a small cot that held his overly fed frame. His breathing was labored and it was obvious he had lost a significant amount of blood.

"Light some wall torches and bring some candles," Odetta bit toward the maidservants, "and some food - at once. Where is the healer?" she asked.

"She went to attend to the birth of the first child of one of your generals. She said she would check in on him in the morning. She said he will live, but will be weak for a while."

"Priest! Priest! Wake up and speak to me," demanded Odetta as she shook the cot with all her might.

Nothing.

"Priest - I mean for you to wake now!"

Silence.

"Hand me that basin," she ordered Naelyn. "Yes - that one," she said as she pointed to the basin on the table near the window; before proceeding to pour its contents all over the man.

With startled eyes, Father MacArtrey raised his head and locked glances with the pagan priestess.

"Tell me, *Father*; why should I not kill you where you lay?" she asked sarcastically.

"Because you need me to locate the scrolls?" he asked sheepishly.

"Nay - that wouldn't be it," she said as she launched a hefty assault across his face. He grimaced and his cheek grew red - the clear outline of her hand mapped across the entire right side of his face.

"Because you have bigger problems on your hands, my lady," he replied confidently and sat up, pushing his feet to the floor beneath him.

"And what would they be, my dear priest?" she asked.

"It has been storming for nearly three days my lady."

"And why would that concern me?" she ventured.

"Because of the curse, of course," he answered.

"What curse?" asked Naelyn.

Odetta's face grew pale. She sat in the chair next to the bed and tapped her fingers on the cot before her. *Could it be? Nay. It's not possible. Possible but not probable.*

"What curse?" Naelyn asked again.

"The storm curse," replied the priest. "The curse we called nearly three fort night's past."

"What am I missing here?" directed Naelyn to Odetta.

"You were not here; you had gone to see to your sister's newest bastard child, Naelyn."

"It was not recorded?" inquired Naelyn.

"Nay. It was. I recorded it with the older scrolls, I have it in my possession." said Father MacArtrey.

"Where?" asked Odetta.

"In a safe place, near my chapel, on O'Malley lands."

* * *

Hot breath on the back of her neck reminded her she was not alone. Her head lay on his long muscular arm and his left forearm gripped tightly about her rib cage. Their legs were entangled under mounds of bed linens and furs and a chill pierced the air as she shivered. Her nipples ached from the cold and she grimaced.

Instantly the fire sparked and rose, heating the room as daylight broke across the wall. He gripped her knee with his left his hand and lazily rubbed his way up her leg towards her hip in circular motions sending spindles of warmth down her spine until they pooled in her center.

This was no monk. *No monk indeed.*

Her gown bunched about her waist and though he wore a night shirt, it would not hide his imposing erection pressed against her backside. She shivered and moaned and instantly his grip about her waist tightened.

How did he get in here?

"You summoned me."

He did not speak, for his mouth was busy nibbling her neck and shoulders while his hand was making promises of things to come. A burning ache rose between her legs which she quickly clenched together.

Impossible.

"Nay."

"You heard me?"

He nodded into her back.

"Have we? Did we? Am I?"

"Shhh…"

"Who are you? What are you?"

"You know who I am."

"How long have you been here - have we been - like this?"

"Shhh… Rest now, my lady."

A thundering knock on the door awakened Darina from her haze. She grabbed the furs and bundled them about her tightly, turning over to find the bed empty, except for herself.

"Not again - I was having the best dream," she wailed.

"It's time to get up my sister," said Dervilla as she marched toward the hearth and added more firewood to the chilly room. We have much to do to finalize the preparations for the feast, the Samhain celebration, and your wedding - I might add."

"Ugh…" Darina replied as she sat up.

"Tell me about this dream," Dervilla said. "You look remarkably sated for one who sleeps alone," she chided. "Don't make me come in there after it," she teased as she pointed an accusing finger at Darina's disheveled hair and tangled night gown.

"You'll do no such thing. Stay out of my head!"

"Very well then, I will expect you downstairs shortly. Ruarc wishes to speak with you. Don't make him wait."

TWENTY - FOUR

O'Malley Strong House - Lucian's Chamber

Lucian had been studying the scrolls for hours. He had even had to call in for extra candles and torches as some of the manuscript was faded and worn and hard to clearly make out. As far as he could tell, there were two languages represented and several codes that needed deciphering - but he had been successful. *How do I explain this to Ruarc?*

Ruarc arrived just as Lucian was rolling up the last of the scrolls and binding them again with the leather ties that had once encased them. Although several wax seals were broken upon their opening, he didn't worry about explaining that to the priest. No - the priest would have plenty of explaining to do himself.

"So - what do you make of those?" asked Ruarc as he sat upon the bench in front of the scribe's table where the scrolls had been laid out. "I couldn't make heads or tails of them, I don't recognize the lettering," said Ruarc.

"Aye - it's a very old language with symbols that haven't been used in years."

"Why do you suppose Father MacArtrey had these in his possession?" Ruarc continued.

"Well - considering the priests history, it doesn't surprise me. You may not remember this, but Father MacArtrey came here seeking shelter over 20 years ago after Odetta Burke claimed the monastery for herself. Many of the monks and priests were killed, but he escaped with his life and a few belongings."

"I seem to remember that. My sister insisted we build a chapel for him and offer him sanctuary."

"Aye."

"Then you are saying these are simply remnants of what he took with him from the monastery?" he asked.

Lucian cleared his throat, straightened his robes and retied the belt fastened about his waist. "In a manner of speaking."

"I don't understand," replied Ruarc, a look of confusion washing over his face.

Lucian rung his hands nervously - unable to find the words. "Yes and no, Ruarc. Yes and no. The scrolls are most definitely from Burke lands and they may have even come from what was left of the monastery - but they do not relate to the Christian god, or the church that Father MacArtrey represents."

"What do you mean? The Monastery on Burke lands has been there nearly a hundred years. What is in those scrolls?"

"They are old, Ruarc, I would assume from the texts that they date back as far as perhaps fifty maybe even a hundred years or more. They contain reiterations of ancient writings that go back further than that though. Ancient pagan witchcraft and demon worship."

Ruarc nodded his understanding. "Druids - like you?" he asked.

Lucian shot Ruarc a warning glance making his unease well known. "Nay. These manuscripts contain records of abductions, human sacrifice, demon summoning, evil curses, plague, pestilence and war - all manner of evil doings. I have seen nothing like it before in my life. The curse of the male offspring that Odetta placed on our lands years ago is recorded inside."

A look of astonished rage boiled over Ruarc's face. "What do you think Father MacArtrey was doing with these scrolls? Why wouldn't he have burned them?" Ruarc rose, grabbed the scrolls from atop the table and strode towards the hearth to extinguish the evil in the fire. Lucian suddenly blocked his path and reached for them.

"Wait!" commanded Lucian. "By the gods - leave them be!"

"Why?" Ruarc asked as he reluctantly handed them back over to Lucian.

"At first, I thought to do the same. Then - I pondered why the priest would have kept them. Perhaps he kept them intact to discern a way to break the curse. Perhaps he kept them and intended to send them to Rome," responded Lucian.

"Aye, they are very old. I would imagine the Vatican would have cause to examine them," Ruarc acknowledged.

"However."

"However?"

"However, as I looked through them - I mean as I said before, they go back years. Long, long, years before. But - there is a recent entry. On the last page of the scrolls - it was written probably this year sometime."

"And only Father MacArtrey knew where the scrolls were - so he would have been the one to make the entry," sighed Ruarc.

"That's my concern, Ruarc. Just how involved is this priest in the contents of the scrolls?"

Ruarc tightened his cloak about him. "'Tis verra cold in here Lucian. May I stoke the fire?"

"Please. I became so involved in examining the texts I haven't had the time to be about my daily chores."

"Could you make out the contents of the last entry?" asked Ruarc.

"Aye. Tell me Ruarc - did you encounter unfavorable weather in your travels to the MacCahan keep?"

"Aye - we did - on MacCahan lands. It stormed the entire time we were there. Indeed - it had stormed for nearly three fort nights prior to our arrival and many cottages were lost from flooding. Even the Laird's wife perished when she was swept out to sea assisting the villagers."

"Then - we must prepare," stated Lucian forlornly.

"Prepare for what?"

"The coming storms."

They had traveled all day through the blinding storms and sounds of thunder. The young boy lay in the back of the cart next to Braeden; who would not let go of his hand. Carbry had helped Mavis tie off her own wound and she had worked feverishly with the boy; offering him food and drink – to no avail.

The color had come back in his face and his wound dressings had finally stopped oozing blood. Patrick had prepared an elixir from herbs he had carried with him and gotten some of that down him; while Mavis made a salve with some others he had brought and used that to quell the bleeding in his wrist. They still hadn't heard him speak but he brightened when he recognized they were going in the direction of O'Malley territory.

"I assume he is from O'Malley clan?" asked Mavis to Deasum.

"Aye. I would imagine so. He appears to acknowledge the direction we are heading."

Carbry lead the group and Patrick followed on Deasum's horse while Deasum manned the cart wagon.

"How m-much f-further do you think?" asked Patrick as they rose to stop at the top of a steep hill just past the last of the streams. Daylight was slowly retreating and Patrick did not wish to stop again. They had been on the road for nearly a fort night - much longer than expected - and what he wouldn't give for a dry place to sleep. *I feel like a dried up prune. I am in dire need of a bath and some good ale.*

"Not more than two hours - maybe three - or so; I think. I would expect we would be met by O'Malley soldiers shortly. We shall cross the border in probably half an hour," he replied.

"Ha-have you a quality h-he-healer?" Patrick inquired glancing back at the boy and Mavis who were both now sleeping beside Braeden.

"We have. She was commissioned some time ago. Our previous healer left several years back. Couldn't seem to get along with our priest."

"Pr-priest?" asked Patrick - now concerned.

"Yes - an unfortunate situation really."

"G-go on."

"We are not a religious people by any means; I wouldn't say. However, we have a chapel and it is attended by a Catholic priest - Father MacArtrey. He came to us over twenty winters back. He was a fugitive of Burke lands. Odetta stormed the monastery and killed all the monks. He came to us for refuge."

"I see," stated Patrick. *Tis unfortunate indeed.* Patrick's last experience with a priest had been a bitter reminder that England's influence on Ireland had brought with it a type of bondage unfamiliar to most. The infiltration of the Catholic Church had nearly driven out all but a few who worshiped the old gods and practiced the old ways. Even then, of the ones left who worshiped the old gods; many were terrified of being found out or being persecuted by the others.

"Is the c-clan - Catholic?" he inquired.

Carbry chuckled and Patrick grew hesitant. "Nay," he replied. "Nay - we offered the priest sanctuary and provided him with a chapel that befits his persuasion. That is all. The Laird's wife held a soft spot for the poor man as he had just lost his home and his friends."

"Ah…"

"Many attend services regularly, and the chapel is used for baptisms, weddings, last rites, and other meetings. However, there are still those that practice the old ways. Lucian is a druid you know."

"Lu-Lucian?" asked Patrick.

"Lucian - the eldest member of our clan. He is the clan scribe and record keeper. He works on the nautical maps and territorial boundaries as well. He is training Dervilla, Darina's younger sister, to follow in his footsteps."

"He is a dr-druid?"

"Yes, he practices the old ways. Many say he is the arch-druid for our region. Although – I've never once spoken of it with him before. I do know he is well educated in herbal matters, and assists the healer quite a lot. I'm really surprised you've never heard of him."

"Wh-why is th-that?" Patrick asked.

"Because if I am not mistaken, his brother lives in MacCahan territory. His name is Airard I believe."

TWENTY-FIVE

O'Malley Castle

Him again. Insolent bastard.

You don't mean it. I believe you've grown fond of my visitations and look forward to seeing me.

"Get out of my head," she said.

There he stood, in all his naked glory – before her fireplace – mere steps from her bed.

"And what do you plan on doing now?" she asked hostilely; knowing full well the manner of his intentions - as they were written all over his – well – his – his intentions were clear.

Move over and let me in, it's awfully chilly tonight.

I'll do no such thing. This is my bed and you are not welcome here.

A wicked grin replaced his seductive glance and he crossed his arms over his chest waiting for her to respond.

"Wait!" She stopped to cover her mouth with the back of her right hand and then shot him an accusing glance. "Did I just say that out loud or did I – I mean – did you – hear me?"

I heard you lass.

By the stars. How did I do that?

You did it because you wanted to, Darina.

How do you know my name? How do you know me? "Excuse me. I wish to speak audibly with you."

Why?

Darina shot up from her reclined position on her bed and pointed a chilled finger in his direction. "You – get out! Now!" With that – he was gone.

* * *

Darina awoke to the sounds of pounding footsteps in the hallways and people moving up and about the stair wells. The familiar creaking of the water trolley outside her windows told her water was being brought up the floors. The sounds of muffled voices mixed with footsteps above her confirmed that someone was in her father's chambers.

By the stars it must be nearly midnight. What on earth is going on?

She hazily peeked about her bed chambers and confirmed to her satisfaction that it was indeed night time. She was alone. The moonlight shined brightly on the eastern wall of her room and lightning flashes peeked across the fireplace. The flame had all but gone out. A thunder clap hastened her waking and she sat up and rubbed her eyes tiredly. *Who in the world is making such a racket?*

No one had been in her Father's chambers since his passing and she wasn't sure who would be going up to his tower at this hour. She set about to find Odhran, surely he would know what was going on.

Too tired to fully dress; she slipped onto her floor on bare feet and in her thin ivory shift. *I'll just peek about the door.* The door to her bedchamber made an ominous creaking sound and she hesitated to open it, as if she were doing something wrong.

What on earth am I hiding for? I'm doing nothing wrong. It's these other discourteous hellions that are making all the noise.

When she had managed to open her door a few inches, she was alarmed at the amounts of people going up and down the stairs and the busyness of the hallway. Although everyone looked to be attempting some form of quiet; none were successful. There were no less than three maidservants bustling about as if the keep were on fire, and several men carrying loaded chests and other belongings. Finally, she saw Deasum in the hallway.

She reached her head around her door, attempting not to display more of her body than necessary. "Deasum," she called. Deasum fidgeted from his post manning the stairs and assisting the maidservants with their heavy packages. He looked around and shrugged his shoulders.

"Deasum!" she said more loudly. "Deasum – over here." She had finally caught his attention and he turned to walk towards her door. "My lady, what are you doing up at this hour?"

"I should ask you the same thing. What is all this noise about?" she inquired.

"Ah – we have just arrived. I mean our guests have arrived; just now – at this late hour. Odhran has set the servants to preparing the master's chambers. Patrick – I mean the Laird, I mean your betrothed; has requested a bath before retiring. He means for Mavis and Braeden to bathe as well before retiring in the adjoining chamber."

"In the adjoining chamber?"

"Aye."

"Well - who is this Mavis and Braeden?"

"Braeden is a boy about eleven summers I believe."

"A boy?"

"Aye - And Mavis is his nurse."

"The boy has a nurse?"

"Aye - a might bonnie lass indeed," he answered with a visible blush flushing his cheeks.

"I've got to see this."

"Nay - you'll do no such thing, Darina. Give them until morn to settle in. You can see them when you break your fast. Now go on back to sleep. We shan't make much more noise tonight. You'll see."

Darina nodded her head and moved to shut her chamber door. Deasum was an ornery cuss and she had no intentions of battling wills with him tonight. *I'll just give them an hour or so and then I'll go see for myself.*

***

Odetta paced back in forth in front of the altar, wringing her hands as if in worry. Smoke billowed from the hearth and filled the air with a putrid aroma which made her eyes burn and water.

"Naelyn! Come see to the fire," she called.

Her maidservant and high cleric joined her near the hearth and added wood and scented pine needles to the fire which she quickly had roaring.

"Well - what did he say?" Odetta asked.

"He said, he can probably remember most of it, but most assuredly will need to retrieve the scrolls from his chapel."

"He did - did he?"

"Aye."

"And what else did he say?"

"He said that he is in need of his spirits as the storms make his bones ache."

"Petulant fool! You tell him he will get no ale, until I have my curse!"

"Nay. 'Tis no reason to shout, my lady," came the reply from the doorway of the storage room looking into the great chamber of the monastery. "I have need of sustenance and drink; and I will tell you what of the curse I can remember," said Father MacArtrey as he strode towards the large table in the middle of the room and sat down as if waiting to be served.

Odetta's mouth dropped open in disbelief at the man's brazen attitude and she mumbled something under her breath.

"Verra well. Naelyn, see he is brought refreshment; and some ale," she said and directed her gaze at the arrogant priest who sat at her table.

"You will tell me what you know - this moment - or you will go below with the others. I will not hesitate to chain you to the stone wall like an animal."

"I ken ye," he replied and nodded, stroking his beard.

"From what I can remember, the curse went something like this,"

> "A curse upon the land is ripening;
> storms of rain, thunder and lightning.
> Wherever the last known male resides;
> the storms shan't stop 'til eventide.
> Upon the winds this curse shall ride;
> and follow the last of the O'Malley pride."

'Til death befalls the cursed eyes;
the last known male shall n'more abide.

"That sounds like it. There may be some small variations but I think you have the most of it," said Odetta as she sat down across the table from the priest.

"Aye," he replied. "That is what you bade me record. It is."

"Odetta," interjected Naelyn, "What does the curse mean?"

Odetta stood and walked towards the hearth, casting a wary glance towards Naelyn was seated at the scribe's bench under the window working on her registry.

"It means nothing – now," she said.

Naelyn rose to stand beside her. "What do you mean it means nothing now? If I understand it correctly, wherever the last O'Malley male is – there will be constant storms."

"Aye. 'Tis what it means indeed," interrupted the priest.

"But it's stopped raining you fool!" shouted Odetta. "Throw him below with the others," she ordered Easal as he entered the great room.

"And what of his food?" asked Naelyn.

"Give it to the dogs."

TWENTY - SIX

O'Malley Castle

Darina grew more impatient by the minute. When she felt it was finally safe to leave her chamber she sunk her feet into her silk slippers and peered around the door. *Good - all clear. Not even a sentry at my door? I see how much value they place on my chamber.* She chuckled at the thought.

O'Malley castle was near impenetrable. There hadn't been soldiers placed at chamber doors in decades. It was nigh impossible to gain entry through the castle doors without being seen, so there was seldom any need for extra security.

After she had made it halfway down the hallway towards the back stairs; she realized she had forgotten her linen robe and was clothed only in her thin shift. "Jaysus! It's cold out here," she muttered under her breath which sent steam pouring into the air. While her first thought was to turn back to her room, she quickly changed her mind when she heard footsteps coming up the third floor stairs. *By the gods, I must look the harlot dressed thus at this hour.*

Seeing no other means of escape, she quickly bounded up the stairs to the fifth floor and spotted light beaming out from underneath the door to her father's masters' chamber. *I'll just take a peek inside.*

Halt.

Darina looked around her for the voice but saw no one. She walked a few steps down the hallway and surveyed the empty stairway. *I must be addled. Too much of that elderberry wine.* She crept back towards the chamber door and made to open it.

Halt.

I know I heard that; didn't I? She pinched herself. *I know I'm awake. There's no one here. I must definitely give up the spirits.*

She opened the door to the chamber slowly and meticulously; lest she make a sound. All the servants had left and Odhran had long since retired, she mused. The fire was burning hot inside the chamber and the window had been thrust open overlooking the balcony atop the battlements. She could hear snoring from the adjoining room and steam rose in her peripheral vision.

Halt. Come no further.

But - no one is here.

Then she saw him. At least two sizes too large for the wooden tub he lay in the bath with his knees atop it and his feet nearly touching the floor. Froth floated atop the water and steam rose, a testament to the heat of it. He lay, she assumed, asleep inside with a linen cloth tossed over his face.

No one indeed.

What? "What?" she asked verbally this time.

Patrick grinned from beneath his wash towel, knowing full well who she was and why she was there. "*This shall be fun,*" he thought to himself.

If you come any closer, I fear you may get wet.

"Who's there?" she asked aloud, but saw no one.

Light snoring interrupted her train of thought and forced her to gaze towards the large bed against the northern wall of the chamber. A young boy slept soundly in the middle of the gigantic goose down mattress, slobbering on the pillow bere.

Unable to contain herself - Darina tip-toed towards the corner of the room, where Patrick lay in the bathing tub. The back of his neck lay on the edge of the tub and his freshly washed hair dripped into a shallow clay vessel Odhran had no doubt laid there for just such a purpose. She reached towards him as if she might try to look under the linen cloth.

Don't.

She hesitated and removed her hand. *I am such an eejit. What am I doing? I am hearing things.*

Don't let your curiosity git the better o'ye.

"Alright - that's it. I've nay lost me mind," she said as she reached for the washing cloth which covered his face.

Before she could touch the wash cloth, a golden muscular arm ascended from the tub and grabbed her about her right wrist spilling water everywhere. She lost her balance in the water and attempted to grab hold of the side of the tub but was unmercifully thrust into the water and on top of the bathing man.

A hearty baritone chuckle rose in her ears as she struggled to right herself atop the tub. Instead, her arms slipped from the sides of the tub and she found herself grasping a large male chest; seated atop him with her knees about his hips. Her eyes met his briefly and she turned away. He could not contain his laughter. The corners of his lips rose and his eyes crinkled while the motion of his laughter continued to spill water upon the floor beside them.

"I wa-warned ye, lass."

A bevy of curses, the likes of which he had never heard, came spewing forth from her luscious pink mouth as she struggled, to no avail, to remove herself both from his grasp and the tub. She was soaked completely through and her thin linen shift left nothing for him to imagine. Her silk slippers held no grasp on the floor of the tub and the best she could do was turn completely backward from him and face the other direction; sitting back down on his chest with a load "swash."

"Wh-why do you sit thus?" he asked, continuing his laughter.

"I am near to soaking through and unfortunately forgot my robe in my chamber. I fear I am next to naked."

"Nay loovee, you are most d-de-definitely n-naked as far as I can tell."

Darina scoffed and crossed her arms over her chest belligerently, as she pulled and fought with her soaking wet gown.

"Be a gentleman - won't you?"

"Ye pierce m-me, my lady. I was but m-mi-minding my own b-business when ye c-came in here and assaulted m-my p-person," he chided.

Even with her back turned completely to him, Patrick could see the heat rising up in her face. And - she could feel the heat rising in him.

"I am - I must return to my chambers."

"Aye. 'Tis a g-good idea," he said.

"Won't you please close your eyes and be a gentleman so that I may remove myself from this - uh - situation?" she whimpered.

"But of course, m-my lady," he started to say as Odhran came charging through the door.

"What on god's green earth are you doing Darina O'Malley?" queried Odhran at the site of her straddling his chest with her backside; seated upright in the tub on top of the new Laird. "You look like a drowned kitten," he said.

"A c-cu-curious kitten, I'm afraid old ch-chap," said Patrick. "It appears t-t-to m-me that she could not wait to m-ma-make my acquaintance," he sputtered through halting laughter.

Odhran grabbed the laird's robe from the peg aside the hearth and stomped towards Darina. "Now get yer soaking wet arse outta that tub there Darina a'for I call for yer aunt Atilde - she willna be happy w'dis at all."

Patrick gulped back a breath in an attempt to contain his amusement and squelched a cringe making it obvious how humored he was by the situation.

"Don't look now Odhran, turn your head," she pleaded.

"Good lord lass, I've seen yer arse more times than I have my own wife's. I did yer swaddling. Never mind now, let's just git ye outta here a'for ye catch yer death."

"I won't l-lo-look," said Patrick. "I p-pr-promise," he continued as he firmly grabbed her hips with both hands and proceeded to lift her up out the tub. She slapped at his arms in mock anger and protestation, hoping it would save her dignity.

Don't play coy with me ye little hellion. I know why you came in here. Pray tell you couldn't wait 'til tomorrow eve - when I've properly wed ye?

"Hold your tongue," she shot back over her shoulder as Odhran held out the robe for her and assisted her from the tub. She held her head high and pranced on as if she were a queen,

unwilling to give the fiend the satisfaction of her
embarrassment.

"What did you say?" asked Odhran.

"What?"

"Why did you tell me to hold me tongue? I said naught," he
replied.

Frustrated, Darina threw up her hands and whispered to
Odhran, "just take me to my room please."

Good night, my lady.

Good night indeed.

TWENTY - SEVEN

O'Malley Castle

Darina woke to an incessant knocking at her door. She quickly surveyed her room and realized it was well past sun up. *How long have I slept?* As she turned to grab her robe she realized it lay on the floor, still soaking wet. A flush rose to her cheeks as she remembered the events that had transpired the night before. She grinned.

"Darina O'Malley, open this door at once," said her Aunt Atilde. "We have much to do this day and I don't care to be kept waiting."

"Hold on," she replied as she rose and searched for her cloak which normally hung on a peg near the fire. *Jaysus, I left it downstairs.* Her hair was damp and unruly from her "bath" the night before and she didn't feel like explaining the condition of her room.

"Whatever is so important that I must be disturbed in this manner?" she asked as she slung open the door to her chamber.

"Girl — don't you speak to me that way. You know I haven't the patience to tolerate one of your moods. Today you are to be wed and there is much to be done," spewed her aunt as she careened into the room.

"Starting with this room," said Odhran as he walked passed Atilde inside with no less than three servants. They quickly began gathering her things and packing her chests.

"What do you think you are doing, Odhran?" she asked over heavy lids that hadn't quite awakened.

"Moving your things, Darina."

"Moving them? Why?"

"Darina, your things are going upstairs to the master's solar. Your room is being set up in the adjoining suite to the Laird's. You are getting married," Atilde cackled out loud. "Have ye forgotten?"

"Nay. I haven't forgotten but why must it be done now?"

"The MacCahan requested thus. Braeden and his nurse, Mavis shall have your chamber now. We are bringing in an extra bed and setting up chests for them, over yonder," pointed Ruarc who stood in the door way.

"You're giving my room to that brute's mistress and his bastard?" she asked stoically.

"Nay. M-Ma-Mavis 'tis not me mistress and Br-Braeden is but me foster, but y-yes, they are to t-take this room," said Patrick from behind Ruarc. Ruarc shot her a stern warning glance and turned to leave Patrick standing there staring at her, still clothed in but a thin shift. She recognized his voice but refused to look at him.

"Cold my l-lady?" he asked glancing at her pert nipples and chuckling before striding to the hearth and raising the fire. Servants continued to work feverishly packing her things and taking them down the hallway.

"Darina, won't ye *please* put some clothes on?" gasped Atilde. Odhran turned and handed her a dry robe from one of her chests and sighed.

"I m-much prefer her th-this way," laughed Patrick before heading towards the door.

221

Ruarc shot her a stern look once last time before heading towards the hallway. "We shall see you for the noon meal shortly?" he half asked half commanded before shutting the chamber door.

* * *

The stench was nearly unbearable - a mixture of sour ale and human waste that assaulted the senses. The pounding on the back of his head had not let up and he feared his ears would burst. His wrist ached and festered and although the bleeding had stopped hours before, he felt weak and knew he had lost too much blood.

"Where am I?" he asked the unresponsive dark.

He pulled his heavy hand to his head and realized he was chained to a stone wall. Turning to move, his legs sloshed through no less than two inches of putrid water.

"Shhh," came the sound next to him. "Quiet."

"Who's there?" asked the priest.

"Quiet," came the response. "Don't make a sound, ye'll wake the rats."

"Rats?" he cried.

"Hush, mon. 'Tis rained again and the rats are up higher in the rock. They won't come down here lest ye make a noise."

"Who are you?" he asked the voice.

"A prisoner like ye. Don't you ken where ye are?"

He attempted to look about him but saw little. Although his eyes began to adjust to the dark, all he could make out were stone walls. "I'm not sure," the priest responded. "Is this hell?"

"Close enough," the chuckle rose and quickly became a hacking cough. "Ye be in the dungeons, a'neath the monastery. Ye are a Burke prisoner. Who are ye?" the voice whispered.

"Father MacArtrcy from O'Malley lands."

"A priest," whispered the voice.

"How long have I been down here?" asked the Father.

"No more n'a day I suppose," the voice responded. "But ye have slept near the entire time."

"And you?"

"Nay - I haven't been able to sleep," replied the voice.

"How long have you been here?"

"A long time. I lost count I think. Might close to ten winters, I s'pose."

"Shite," the priest swore. "And what is your name?"

"Ah – I'm Cordal – Cordal McTierney."

TWENTY - EIGHT

O'Malley Castle - The Great Hall

Darina took her time getting dressed for the noon meal. After all, she was no longer in her own chamber. Her belongings had been brought to the adjoining room of her father's former solar. Everything was there, her two chests which contained her clothing and personal items. Her wall hangings, which were beautiful tapestries of sunsets and falcons, her red and gold settee lounge chair her father had gotten her for her birthday and the beautiful Indian rug her merchant friend Sanjay had given her as well. Even her weapons and shield were hung above the hearth and her writing utensils sat on the corner table near the window.

Indeed, everything was there. Everything except her bed.

"A might presumptuous of him isn't it?" she muttered softly.

"What did ye say dear?" asked her aunt Atilde who was putting the finishing touches on her hair.

"I asked where my bed was" she replied.

Atilde laughed a hearty laugh and straightened the O'Malley clan brooch upon her shoulder where she had clasped the plaid. The brooch was a fine and intricate piece of work. A regal looking dragon with eyes of red rubies surrounded by a sun made of amber and a moon of sapphire centered upon a circular crest of mistletoe.

"My dear, ye've no need of a bed of your own, you are geeting mewried t'day."

"Then am I to be forced to share *his* bed?"

Nay.

"What did you say?" asked Darina.

"Naught," replied her aunt shaking her head.

I'll nay force ye. But ye shall - just the same.

A flush rose over Darina's face and she clenched her fists tightly.

"Get out of my head!" she shouted.

Atilde turned her by the arms to look her straight in the eyes. "What on earth is wrong with you? Had you too much wine last eve?"

"Nay."

"Darina, I ken you are a wee bit anxious me dearie, but ye must get ahold'a yerself."

Darina hung her head and nodded her acknowledgement.

"All done. Now come on down to the hall and break yer fast with the rest'a us. I'm sure yer betrothed wishes to get a good look at ye. What a mighty fine bride ye'll make me dearie, yer mam would be so proud of ye."

Atilde gathered her satchel and headed towards the door. "Aye. I'll be down in a moment," she said and caught a glimpse of herself in the looking glass.

Beautiful.

"I know you can't see me so stay out of my head I said," she spoke to the air around her.

"I can see you fine my sister, and I assure you I am not in your head," said Dervilla from the doorway that lead from the main solar to the adjoining sitting room now occupied by Darina's belongings.

"What's wrong with you anyhow? You are behaving most peculiarly."

"There's nothing wrong with me."

"Wedding jitters then?"

"Nay. I don't have any jitters to speak of Dervilla," responded Darina straightening her plaid and picking at her hair.

"Something's amiss here. Let me see - something is missing. What could it be?" she asked walking around the room. "I know," she turned and faced Darina.

"What?" responded Darina rolling her eyes.

"The bed," responded Dervilla erupting with wicked laughter.

"Ha. Ha. Aren't you the funny one, Dervilla?" she said.

"So - tell me what he looks like," whispered Dervilla. "Go on - is he handsome?"

"I have no idea."

"What? You haven't met him yet?"

"Not really."

"What does that mean? I heard there was an incident last night," said Dervilla openly picking at her.

Darina clenched her fist and ground her teeth. "By the goddess! Who told you?"

Dervilla could not contain her amusement and doubled over with laughter. When she had finally contained herself, she rose and faced Darina.

"You mean to say ye bathed with the man, who was no doubt naked as the day he was born, yet ye don't know what he looks like?"

"I did'na bathe with him! I simply went into the solar to see what all the fuss was about and he was asleep in the tub with a cloth over his face. I saw his long hair dripping over the tub. I could see that he was a very large – I mean – a tall person and when I reached to remove the cloth over his face – I tripped."

"And fell into the tub?"

"Yes – I fell into the tub. But I kept my eyes closed and then I turned around so as not to permit him to see my wet – form."

"Your wet form?"

"Yes. All I had on was me shift."

Dervilla's face turned four shades of purple. "You sat on him? With your back turned to him? By the stars! That is the funniest thing I have ever heard. Are ye sure ye didn't take just a little peek?"

"Yes I'm sure. Besides Odhran came in to assist me out of the tub; I mean the situation, and I returned to my room."

"Did ye anger him?"

"Perhaps."

Nay.

"Stop it," said Darina.

"Stop what?" asked Dervilla.

"Nothing."

"Darina - who are ye talking to? Ye've been talking to yourself for a few days now and I fear ye've gone mad."

"No one. I must be hearing things."

"What are ye hearing sister?"

"Someone, speaking in my head. Like ye do sometimes."

"Well - it's not me."

"I know that."

"How do you know?"

"Because it's not your voice Dervilla."

"Whose voice is it Darina?" Dervilla asked nervously.

Darina's cheeks flushed and turned away from Dervilla as if she were working on tidying up.

"Darina."

Silence.

"Darina! I asked ye a question. Whose voice is it?"

"His."

"His who?" Dervilla asked again. "The MacCahan?" Dervilla gasped and clutched her mouth. "How do ye know? Have ye heard him speak?"

"Yes, last night for a brief moment when Odhran was helping me out of the - situation," she replied.

"And he sounded the same as in your head?"

"Yes and no."

"What does that mean Darina?"

"When he speaks in my head, he does not - ugh - stammer."

"Why would you let him into your head? Why would he be speaking to ye with his mind? I don't understand what is going on here." Dervilla grabbed her sister by her forearms and shook her.

"Darina, ye have to *let* him communicate with ye that way. You have to have a strong bond with a person before they can speak through your mind. And ye have to *permit it*. Ye can deny them access. And - ye've never met him."

Aye, ye have.

"Aye, I have Dervilla," she responded shaking her head up and down in agreement.

"What do ye mean Darina? You're not making any sense."

"The monk. The one that took care of me while I was sick."

"The man ye said ye saw in your chamber? The one who fed ye and chanted over ye? What about it? Ye were delirious Darina, with the fever."

"Nay. It was him."

"Him who?"

"My betrothed Dervilla, Patrick MacCahan."

* * *

Vynae had worked tirelessly all night keeping watch over the injured boy and applying herbs to his wounds. She had managed to get most of the tonic down him and a little broth and he was regaining the color in his face. Lucian had stopped by several times to see to him and pray and even brought Dervilla once and together they chanted and hummed while he slept.

Deasum had laid him in the third chamber on the left in the clan's sick house. The clan was blessed to have a fully functioning sick house complete with five separate chambers and two large halls. Vynae's healing abilities were known far and wide and many of the women of the clan had taken to birthing their bairns in the sick house rather than at home.

Lucian saw to it that she had an apprentice and more than enough supplies; including various herbs, roots and plants that had been used for hundreds of years. Father MacArtrey had spoken his peace about the methods she used; but he created no fear in Vynae. She would not be moved. Her craft was ancient and laden with mysticism, but she was no witch; and no lecher of a priest was going to tell her how to tend to her duties.

"How fairs the boy this morning?" asked Lucian, peeking his heard through the chamber door.

"He is doing well Lucian. I think he may rise soon. He has taken to the tonic and had nearly two mugs of broth," she replied. "Although - I think he preferred mead over all else."

Lucian chuckled and walked to his bedside. "You're stitching is excellent. I don't think he will bear much of a scar there," he said pointing to the boy's wrist which was freshly packed with a salve over his wound. "Have you any idea who he is?"

"Nay. But I've sent for Murchadh; he should know. There are at least three wee ones still missing from last harvest -all boys. Surely, someone will know who he is."

"I hope so. If not, Gemma will find a lass on the island to foster him - I'm sure."

"Do you ken this is the work of the Burke's?" he asked.

"Aye - it would appear so. They shaved his head. I fear what their plans were. That is normally done only for sacrifice. His wound was not deep, so I'm not sure what interrupted them, but something did. The goddess was looking after him - I would say."

TWENTY - NINE

O'Malley Castle

Darina sat in her settee lounge chair long after Dervilla had left. She was troubled - irritated really. It had rained non-stop all night and still continued to storm. She had hoped to be married atop the peek overlooking the bay; but the weather would not permit. Even if it stopped pouring now, the grounds were too wet and would no doubt be muddy. Her Uncle had instructed that the private banqueting hall on the fifth floor near her father's chambers be prepared for a private ceremony with family and close friends at sundown.

The reception would be downstairs in the great hall and would no doubt continue outside near the bonfires to be lit in celebration of Samhain. Lucian would perform the service and Minea was to bring the crucifix and holy water from the chapel.

Father MacArtrey's cleric, Galen, would pray a Christian prayer and bless the union.

It was a suitable alternative she acknowledged. *Not how I pictured it though.* Servants had worked tirelessly throughout the morning preparing the banqueting hall. Even now she could smell the fragrant aroma of flowers and lavender scented candles the chandler had brought from England as it floated down the hallway.

She rose and walked into the main solar and towards the balcony that over-looked the western side of the bay. From there, she could see the ships that had brought in the guests for the celebration as well as a myriad of tents that sat next to the inn and guest cottages. The grounds were a bustle of activity, in spite of the storms.

It was an important time. The O'Malley alliance with the MacCahan's was good not only for her people, but the surrounding clans as well. The MacTierneys - whose clan lay just to the south of the O'Malley territory - enjoyed a long and prosperous alliance with the clan. As did the Montgomery's who were just to the east.

She breathed a deep sigh and turned to survey what was to become her new chamber. Her father's bed was all that remained of his belongings now. Even the wall hangings had changed as the MacCahan had brought his own tapestries. Some of the finest weapons she had ever seen hung above the hearth. Ruarc had told her they were the workmanship of her betrothed. Evidently, he was a skilled artisan and blacksmith.

The bed linens had changed as well. *Another gift from Sanjay no doubt.* Beautiful red and gold brocade material with golden tassels adorned the bed along with golden bed curtains and red silk sheets. It was beautiful and matched her settee perfectly.

There were two large chests on either side of the bed and the most enormous bathing tub she had ever seen sat just feet from the hearth. Beside the tub was a privacy screen matching the bed linens. A bench with golden padding now sat at the foot of the bed making it easier to dress. Her wedding dress hung on the peg beside the hearth and new golden silk slippers lay on the floor underneath.

She plopped down on the bench and rested her elbows on her knees. *I should be happier about this.* Darina had never thought to marry. At nineteen summers, she had passed the normal marrying age. Most girls her age were married and swollen with child at fifteen; but not the O'Malley women. There weren't enough men to go around. She had all but resigned herself from marriage when her parents' deaths threatened her station.

It was her heart that worried her the most. She had lost the most important people to her in a matter of moons and she feared the possibility of further loss. She had given her body to a man once in vain, she was not about to give her heart away.

I'll nay hurt you lass.

The brief interruption of her thoughts reminded her she was woefully late for the noon meal. "Ruarc will have my head," she thought out loud as she raced down the hallway towards the stairs.

* * *

Murchadh and Kyra stood stoically overlooking the grounds from the high tower of the castle, completely soaked through. The storms had not relented a bit and their armor grew heavy with rain.

Everyone was on alert and all of the soldiers were on guard today. The clan was preparing a celebration and the honored guests would be protected as was befitting the O'Malley clan honor. Sentries were stationed nearly everywhere and the bay guards were extra careful with all the vessels having sent the dogs to inspect each one before permitting their docking.

238

The bridges were drawn and only let down upon orders of Murchadh, Kyra or Ruarc himself. It was nearly impossible to gain entry at this point.

"Are ye to attend the wedding Murchadh?" she asked.

"Nay - me wife Olonea shall. I shall remain in the tower. Carbry will take me place for the reception and then we shall switch about half way through I s'pose."

An ominous screech bellowed overhead and they quickly saw what Riann was announcing. In the distance, just over the peek rode at least fifty men towards the keep.

"Can ye make out who it is?" she asked.

"Aye," he replied. "They wave the MacCahan banner and they wear the plaid. 'Tis our Laird's brother Payton and his men; just as the missive said."

"I hadn't expected them so soon. They must have made good time," she replied.

"I'd guess they didn't meet with ill weather. Why don't you go below and have the bridges drawn and meet them. I'll send for Atilde to make arrangements for their keeping."

"Aye," she replied and headed for the stairs.

THIRTY

O'Malley Territory

Darina secured the chamber door and scurried down the
hallway to the stairs. She nearly knocked over a handful of
servants carrying barrels of honey wine into the banqueting
hall. She tripped over a cart and knocked over a candelabrum as
she flew down the stairs towards the great hall. After stubbing
her toe on a tray that had been set out on the third floor
balcony she turned the corner to the stairwell which opened up
over the great hall overlooking the clan dais and the hearth.

The hall was full and bustling with activity; yet the dais
remained empty and her father's chair was barren. *Where are
they? Surely they haven't left.*

She slowed her pace and attempted to catch her breath while
pushing a loose tendril of curly red hair behind her right ear.
Her heart was beating so fiercely she was sure the whole keep

could hear it. She stopped for a moment to gain her composure and started down the stairs again, one at a time at a reasonable rhythm.

Her uncle Ruarc awaited her below. She had much to say to the new laird and little time to do it before their vows would be taken. Dervilla walked briskly by and took her seat on the platform and waived for Darcy to join her.

When she reached the bottom stair, her uncle took her hand and swung it behind him to his left. "Darina, this is Patrick MacCahan, soon to be Laird Patrick O'Malley, your betrothed." She caught a gulp in her throat and examined her tiny hand which now lay inside the larger one.

"My lord," she responded as she quickly tipped her head down and smiled while he led her towards the dais to their seats. "Did I understand my uncle correctly? You intend to take the O'Malley name?"

"I d-do," he said as seated her to his left and then took the Laird's regal looking chair.

"We were expecting you much sooner," scowled Ruarc who sat to his right. "We have been waiting quite a while."

"'Twas well worth the w-wait," corrected Patrick. "You are st-stunning," he whispered to her under his breath.

Darina blushed and straightened her skirts. She fiddled with her hair and the cloth on the table, and then straightened her chair again.

Relax - 'tis your home. I am the one who should be anxious.

She blew out a long held breath slowly and then turned to her right to finally face and rebut him. He was turned away speaking with Ruarc; and the boy who had come with him was standing beside his chair, pulling at his arms and yanking at his newly woven braids.

His skin cast an almost ethereal hue about him and his brown shoulder length hair carried golden streaks throughout. A braid adorned each side of his temple clasped off with golden bands and it bespoke his station as a warrior. His left hand grasped an iron goblet full of mead which seemed tiny in comparison.

The great hall was filled to capacity and maidservants and village women skipped from the kitchens and between tables filling trays with meat and baskets with warm bread. Their intentional stares at Patrick were not lost on Darina. She was dizzy with anxiety. It seemed as if every eye in the room was on him - or was it on *her*?

This alliance meant the world to her uncle and she knew her people were relying on her good sense and O'Malley pride to ensure the union was a prosperous one. Her mind wandered. *What if I am not a good wife? What if I can't bear him a son? What if I displease him?*

"*'Tis not possible, kitten. You are lovely beyond measure,*" he spoke to her mind as his left hand sat down the goblet and reached to pat her knee.

A blush arose in her face and she playfully slapped her hand on his left knee without thinking and loudly stated, "Stop that."

Dervilla punched her with her elbow and scrunched her eyebrows together as if questioning her. Braeden turned to look at her and Patrick followed suit. "She's a wee bit of a hell cat isn't she, Patrick?" Braeden asked giggling.

"Nay," he said. "She's an a-an-angel Braeden," he replied and locked eyes with her.

Darina froze. She held her breath. She choked on it. Her eyes widened as if she were about to become the victim of a hideous crime and she felt the hair on the back of her neck stand on end.

It IS you. I knew it.

It was him; the monk that had kept to her bedside when she was ill. Tall, muscular, dark with green eyes the color of newborn grass and a comfortably warm chiseled knee as well. *By the gods, I'm still touching his knee! Get ahold of yeself. Ye look a fool.*

His face lit up and he grabbed her hand under the table, then brought it to his mouth and kissed her palm. His lips were moist and warm and the sensation of his mouth on her hand caused her stomach to jump. He rubbed his stubble over her hand and bent his head lower to travel below her wrist. Braeden squirmed and feigned illness and Darina turned bright red. Her sisters grew silent in watch and the air grew thick.

"Are ye hu-hungry, my lady?" he asked.

She nodded a receptive yes and he began to fill her plate with the choicest meats at the table and added aged cheese, bread and plum sauce. He made sure she was served and ate first. Braeden eventually wormed his way to a seat at the table and sat between Patrick and Ruarc.

Darcy leaned over and whispered in her ear. "He looks just like Da doesn't he?" she asked.

Dumbfounded, Darina replied. "Patrick looks nothing like Da, what are you talking about?"

Darcy nodded towards the other side of the table. "No – him," she replied pointing at Braeden.

* * *

Father MacArtrey had finally dozed off when the sound of heavy footsteps and clanking metal above announced a visitor was heading down to the dungeons. Cordal clinched his chains about him and skittered towards the darkest corner he could reach. The rain had been stopped for nearly a day. Although there remained no standing water; the odor of urine and mildew permeated the air.

Easal's second in command, Rufus, stomped down the wooden stairway and raised a lantern overhead to examine the chamber. He turned his nose at the stench and squelched a retch as bile rose in his throat.

"Where is the priest?" he shouted overhead to no one in particular, holding his nose. Father MacArtrey cringed. *This is it. They are going to gut me.*

He kicked the wall with his boot and shouted again, "Where is the bloody priest?"

Chains rattled and prisoners scurried as close to the safety of darkness as they could; yet no answer could be heard.

"I'll ask one more time and then I'll get after ye - each one of ye - one at a time until I have that priest."

"I am he," the priest said and stretched to as far as he could stand, still attached to the chains that bound him to the stone wall. "Please don't hurt anyone a'cause o'me."

Rufus raised the lantern and shown it in the face of Father MacArtrey. It was a lined, scarred and tired - aged face indeed. No doubt he had seen too much in his years and would see much more.

"Have ye come to kill me?" he asked.

Rufus shook his head in answer and replied, "Nay. I haven't come to kill ye mon. Mayhap ye should pray for death though. I'm sure ye will seek it after Odetta gets through wit ye."

THIRTY - ONE

O'Malley Territory

Thankfully the storms had stopped. The sun had peeked out of the clouds and was creating a fog of steam the closer she came to the peeks. Although she was damp - Kyra was not completely soaked through. Her boots were covered in mud, her chain was heavy upon her tunic and truis and her helmet was making her neck ache. Soon she would be done with her duties and be able to bathe and dress for the ceremony at sun down.

She instructed the guards to leave the bridges down and the gates at ready to receive the soldiers from MacCahan territory. Atilde was busy readying the dome tents for their keep and the kitchens in the inn were just as busy as the castle to ensure enough food for all the guests.

Riann kept pace with her and sometimes led the way, flying high, back and forth between the men and Kyra's steed. She brought the O'Malley banner with her and could visibly make out the MacCahan banner as she approached the riders.

Atop a large black horse sat who she assumed was Payton, the Laird's brother. Long black hair trailed behind him and he wore a breast plate, cloak and a tartan was draped about his waist. The smooth muscles of his thighs gripped the horse flesh as he rode. He resembled a Roman guard *or god*? She couldn't be sure. Tall and lean with rippled muscles vibrating with the horse's canter. He mesmerized her with his form. Blue eyes stared at her from beneath the banner and she felt her heart jump.

She gulped to suppress a sigh as she neared the travelers. They slowed to a halt in an effort to converse and the front three riders met her midway. Payton first, then what appeared to be his second and third in charge.

"MacCahan?" she asked in the gruffest voice she could muster.

"Aye," he nodded. "I am Payton MacCahan and this is Joducus," he said pointing to the blonde on his right. "This is Vitus," he announced pointing to a burly looking red headed man sitting atop the knurliest horse she had ever seen.

"Shall we go?" she asked hoping they would require no information of her.

"Nay," responded Payton casually.

"Nay?" she asked, lowering her voice.

"Nay, we wish to bathe before passing the walls. Might there be a river or stream close by? My men require little else."

She nodded her head in understanding and rose to point northwest towards the Gelyi River. "If ye turn towards the forest there and travel northwest but for a few moments, ye will encounter the river."

"Good," he said. "I've no wish to witness my brother's union smelling like a hound," he chuckled. "And, Joducus won't be happy 'til Vitus is properly bathed," he said as he smacked Vitus's right arm with his left.

"I'll stand guard here," she offered. "And bring ye when ye be done."

"Nay. Ye will take us, let us be off now," he insisted and turned his horse.

By the goddess what am I going to do now? I can't bathe with the men!

When they finally approached the river, she signaled with her hands for the men to dismount and tie their horses. She remained atop her steed and fiddled with her chain walking her horse back towards the tree line nervously.

"A might strange lad there Payton, wouldn't ye say?" asked Joducus.

"A little more than a might strange," answered Vitus as he hung his tartan on a branch and tip toed into the chilly slow-flowing river.

"I see Patrick in this," said Payton.

"What do you mean," asked Joducus.

"Look – they've sent a wee boy dressed as a soldier to meet us. He's plying us with his folly."

"No doubt he has some mischief to engage in – that's why he remains behind," interjected Vitus already halfway submerged in the river.

She turned towards the river at the wrong moment. Her eyes – still hidden under her helmet – met bare flesh; as an untold number of stark naked MacCahan warriors traipsed to the river bed and began their assault on the water. Splashing, laughter and loud conversation interrupted her mind when she realized she stared in amazement.

"Payton, he seems almost uncomfortable to be here."

"Aye - he does," replied Payton fully clothed and still grooming his horse. "I fear he is up to no good. Why don't you go get him and throw him in?" Payton asked Joducus with an evil grin on his face.

"I think I will," he laughed and discarded his shirt and boots as he strode towards her wearing only his tartan.

Kyra froze in fear. *Saint Brigit - what is he doing?*

"Might I be of some assistance?" she asked lowering her voice as far as she could.

"Why, yes ye can. Yes ye can," Joducus replied and pulled her off the horse. "Join us - won't you?" he said and proceeded to drag her across the ground towards the river. Her heavy muddy boots became entangled with wet ground and she tripped; falling roughly in the mud.

She was now completely covered in it and her chain mail stuck to her tunic and truis. She could barely see two feet in front of her - the mud had caught in her helmet. Laughter could be heard coming from the river; and her assailant had doubled over in delight, pointing at her.

I'll just have to get up and wash my face and helmet off at the riverside and mayhap they will leave me be?

She rose slowly from the ground. She looked a sight. Her hands grasped great balls of earth and she did her best to clear her vision. She staggered towards the river and knelt to bend down when she heard heavy footsteps gaining ground towards her.

Please no!

It was too late, with one mighty push of his foot on her backside; Payton had sent her diving into the freezing cold river; chain mail, helmet and all.

Shouts erupted and gurgled laughter could be heard from under the water. She struggled to breathe but couldn't as her chain mail and helmet were weighing her down. She had no choice but to remove her helmet and chain mail while still under the water. She watched as they traveled slowly to the surface and down the moving river.

"Where is he?" asked Payton growing concerned when she hadn't surfaced yet. "I dinnae know," replied Vitus in shock.

"Find him!" screamed Payton. "Me brathair will have me head if I've killed his wee soldier!"

Soon all the men were diving under water searching for her and flaying their arms about wildly. Payton dived head first into the river to where she had entered. When his hand felt her tunic he grabbed her by the hair and half pulled her to shore. She struggled against him and cursed. *He thinks I'm drowning.*

When they both collapsed on the muddy ground, he rolled her over to inspect her and gasped audibly. "'Tis a lass," he shouted in astonishment.

Joducus left the river, quickly draped himself with his tartan and tore across the ground to where she laid soaking wet and muddy.

"What is the meaning of this?" a stern voice demanded. Payton turned to see Ruarc riding towards the water's edge. He had no doubt seen everything.

He stepped down from his horse and drew his sword as a warning. "What are you doing to my daughter?" he demanded.

Payton stood, raised his palms and surveyed the scene. Kyra lay on the shore of the river, soaking wet and muddy and panting for breathe. Nearly fifty naked men surrounded them, all having bathed in the river and Payton and Joducus stood over her.

"Ruarc," he replied. "Good to see ye, again."

"Don't change the subject," Ruarc instructed and circled towards Payton with his weapon pointed at him. "What are you about?"

"I'm fine father," Kyra mumbled. "'Twas an accident." She rose on her elbows to rub the back of her head and held her hand out for Joducus to help her up.

"Ye don't look fine, Kyra," he replied.

"We had no idea she was a lass," responded Vitus now fully clothed.

"Silence," Ruarc commanded. "You," he said tipping his head to Payton, "explain yourself."

"We thought she was a wee soldier sent by my brother to play us," said Payton. "I dinnae know she was a lass, and would not have behaved thus if I had."

"Yet ye would have no problem treating any O'Malley soldier, youth or otherwise, thus?" asked Ruarc, openly offended.

"I ken what you're saying, my lord," Payton replied dejectedly. "And I beg your pardon and that of your lovely daughter," he added as he bowed towards Kyra and took her hand to kiss it. She didn't know whether to blush or punch him.

By now, all the MacCahan men had managed to re-dress and mount their horses awaiting instructions to leave.

"We'll discuss this further with the Laird," Ruarc stated matter-of-factly and turned to assist Kyra with her horse. "Now – let us be off."

THIRTY - TWO

Burke Territory

"Dunk him in the well water. I'll speak with him after he's had a bath. And you!" Odetta shouted, "Bring him some food and ale." Easal grabbed the priest about the neck and drug him outside to the back of the monastery, throwing him into the water tank.

"Use this," he said as he tossed him some lilac soap and a washing cloth. Naelyn is fetching a monk's robe for you. It's not what you're accustomed to, but it will do for now; at least until your clothes have dried."

"What is going on?" asked Father MacArtrey. "Why wash me if she intends to kill me?"

Easal let loose a guttural laugh and walked towards him. "She has nay intention of killing ye yet, my fine sir," he said and pushed his head back down under the water.

"Odetta has plans for you."

"Plans? For me?"

"Aye - there is the matter of the sacrifice ye ruined; and the scrolls."

Rufus walked past them towards the external entry to the dungeons carrying a young boy who appeared to have been unconscious either by a blow to the head or an elixir - he couldn't be sure.

"There he is Father, the new sacrifice. You get to try that again tonight at Samhain."

"Samhain - 'Tis pagan witchcraft, I shan't do any such thing. You may kill me now."

"Aye. I'd like to, but Odetta insists we need ye."

***

Darina had taken a small nap at the request of her Aunt Atilde. Minea now insisted that she walk about the grounds since the weather was nice and hadn't been for a while. "T'will calm ye nerves, my lady," she insisted.

She strode down to the third floor landing and out the balcony doors that overlooked the armory and practice fields. The sun was clear in the afternoon sky and there was no rain in sight. She could still smell the fuchsia flowers that were hung in the private banqueting hall and yearned for a bit of the elderberry wine. *Just a little bit.*

She leaned over the wall and picked a sprig of Algerian ivy off the stone surface. She twisted it and placed it behind her right ear before licking her lips in remembrance of the wine.

Her sister, Daenal, had made some of her delightful pastries and had taken them up to the banquet room for the reception. She would have skinned her alive had she known Darina scurried out of the hall with a plate full of them; hoping not to be seen.

"I th-thought you m-might like some of th-this," came Patrick's voice from behind her. She turned to face him and he handed her a silver goblet the contents of which smelled like elderberry wine.

"Thank you very much," she responded and took a small sip.

"W-we've only a f-few hours now," he reflected out loud and took a sip from his own goblet as he looked over the grounds and towards the sea.

"Aye," she said and nodded in response. "I see they've moved all yer belongings to the chamber."

"And y-yo-your's as well," he said, setting his wine down on the stool near the railing.

"I saw," she said solemnly, turning away.

"What t-tr-troubles you, D-Darina?"

"'Tis naught - no need to even speak of it."

He moved forward and wrapped his arms around her placing one on each side of her on the railing. She could feel his breath on the back of her neck and heat rose in her stomach. With his left hand he carefully moved her hair behind her and over her left shoulder.

"Tell me wh-wha-what it is, and mayhap I c-can f-fix it," he whispered into her ear sending chills down her spine and causing her to shake.

"D-do I fr-frighten ye lass?" he asked tenderly. His right hand began a trail of light circles up her wrist and continued up her arms, while his left hand now molded to her hip and reached around her stomach.

"Nay," she replied and escaped his arms turning her back to him. "Nay, I don't frighten so easily," she responded and moved to lean against the stone of the castle behind them.

He retrieved her goblet and handed it to her once again.

"Ye mean to ply me with spirits do ye?" she asked abruptly, the seriousness showing in her face. "Will that make me a more congenial mate ye s'pose?"

Her tone startled him. He couldn't be sure if she was jesting or sincere. "I've n-never, I w-wo-would never…I am an h-ho-honorable mon."

"Are you a mon fond of the spirits, Patrick?" she asked and held out her hand to his face to feel the warm, soft texture of his whiskers.

He grabbed her hand and kissed her palm, before abruptly dropping it. It grazed the stone wall behind her as she continued her accusatory glare. She hadn't removed her eyes from his since he handed her the wine.

"You needn't w-wo-worry, luv; I'm n-no-not a drunkard and n-ne-either am I a lecher."

"I've heard otherwise," she accused and pushed her bony right index finger into his chest accusingly. The look of confusion on his face was apparent but quickly turned to irritation.

"Ye've heard wh-what exactly?" he asked raising his voice in frustration and lowering his head closer to hers, never taking his eyes off her.

"I know the way of men," she replied looking down. "And I ken ye are no different." She deepened her glare on him. "A Laird's son ye are, I've no doubt ye've had yer way with the maids; and used whatever…" she raised her left hand to him, still holding the wine and gesturing with it, "methods ye need to make them more affable I presume."

"And wh-why would you pre-presume such about me?" he asked quietly, now resting his forehead on hers.

"You need some way to seduce them I would imagine."

He laughed; a deep subdued gurgled laugh that rose up his belly to his chest and made his body quiver.

"Ye laugh?" she said angrily.

"Aye – I d-do," he replied.

What troubles ye sweets?

Her eyes grew large in anger and she pushed against him but was locked under his grip. Both of her hands were now above her, facing palm up against the stone of the castle; while each of her wrists were gripped by his large hands on either side of her head.

"Don't do that!"

"Wh-why?"

"It's not fair. I don't want you speaking to me that way; don't trespass my mind again."

I will and we will get to the bottom of this.

"What does that mean?" she asked back in her head.

His eyes grew more intense and his forehead pressed harder against hers.

I will find the truth of what bothers ye, and we will be done with this – for good.

He searched her eyes; deep beautiful green eyes that were now pooling with the threat of tears. She drew her breath in tandem with his and her chest rose in synchronicity. He could feel her pulse in her wrists and it quickened. His heart beat was near audible and he felt it in his ears. It seemed that time stood still.

Patrick released his tight bond with her forehead and bent to her ear. "Da-Darina, speak to m-me," he begged.

The warmth of his breath on her ear was more than she could stand. Goose bumps rose on the back of her neck and he felt her pulse increase again in her wrists. She quivered and sucked in a deep breath, feigning struggle with him.

He returned his forehead to hers and searched her eyes. He released her left wrist and rested his right hand securely on her hip. She jumped at the familiarity but edged closer to him anyway.

His left hand loosed her other wrist and framed her cheek. She was magnificent; all spirit and sprite. Beautiful, intelligent, bull-headed and tempting as the day was long. He sighed.

I see I shall pay for my sins with you.

She shook her head against his and attempted to push him off her.

"Ye h-he-heard that?" he asked sheepishly.

"Aye," she replied audibly.

"I did not intend for you to hear that. I apologize for my disrespect," he spoke to her mind.

I heard it nonetheless. I am sorry ye are stuck with a woman such as I. Ye must have angered the gods.

Nay loovie; ye are a gift from the gods.

Why would ye say that?

Because ye can hear me; even when I intend for ye not. Which means — I can hear ye when ye intend me not.

"I don't believe you," she said angrily. "Ye have learned the ways of reading people, ye are but toying with me. No doubt, ye've had much experience using this tool of yers - on the women, no doubt."

He returned his attentions to her neck. He could feel her heartbeat against his stubble. He lazily grazed the side of her face and felt the warmth envelope her as heat rose and a blush adorned her cheeks.

He was close now. Dangerously close to her lips, and if he didn't stop now, she wasn't sure she could deny him.

Ah, but I do love the kissing. Oh please no, don't do this to me now. I haven't the strength…

Her thoughts were interrupted by the taste of his mouth firmly pressed against her lips. His soft whiskers tickled her lips and he kissed a trail around her face; her chin, her cheeks, a peck on her nose - and then back to her lips. She lost her footing and slipped but he quickly grabbed her about the waist and held her firmly against him. His eyes met hers and demanded her involvement.

He bent his mouth to hers again and she lifted her face to join. The taste of honey and mead bathed her tongue as he grasped the back of her neck - his hand caressing her long curly hair. She moved her arms to stabilize herself against the wall but found them instead wrapped around his neck. After what seemed an eternity, he lifted his head from her mouth and returned his forehead to hers.

"*Please don't,*" she begged him with her mind, twisting her head against his in revolt. "*'Tis not fair. A woman should have leave of her private thoughts.*"

You are not any woman, Darina. You are to be my wife, and lady of this castle. If we are to form a proper unification, there should be no secrets between us. There should be no reason ye fear me, lass.

Tears of humiliation rose in her eyes and all the color in her face dissipated. To save her dignity he removed his forehead and placed both arms around her in a tight hug. To his surprise, she clutched him back, squeezing harder than he.

He searched her mind and touched her soul. Flashes of moments in her life raced across his vision. Her father no doubt, laying sick in a bed and succumbing to his weakness; the burial service for her mother. Comforting and caring for her grief stricken sisters who had taken to their beds.

The visions stopped abruptly for a moment. Then they returned; somehow having rewound themselves to a particular moment in time. Her as a girl, perhaps eight or nine winters old, pacing the great hall in distress. Screams of agony filled the air and her father sat in front of her on a bench clenching his fists in his hair. It was her mother. Her younger sisters sat in front of her lined up against the bench in a row, holding hands and whimpering.

266

Lucian ran down the stairs and summoned her Da. Loud whispers she couldn't make out came from the hallway and the healer went running out the front door with a bundle in her arms trailing blood behind her.

A baby – a stillborn girl. Her sister's cries grew louder and Da turned pale. She stopped her pacing and the life drained from her face. *"My fault"*, she thought and turned to run from the keep.

Patrick's visions were interrupted by the feel of hot tears on his chest. She murmured and lowered her eyelashes in shame. He gripped her tighter, giving her no indication he had traversed her thoughts. His right thumb trailed a pattern down her cheek catching the tears in his hand.

A strong thought broke through almost as if she intended it.

The bed – where is my bed?

"The bed?" he inquired tipping his head, not sure if she was aware of their dialogue.

There is only one bed; two chambers and one bed.

He stepped backwards a pace and held her at arm's length. "We have n-ne-need of only one b-bed. We are to b-be m-ma-married."

She raised her eyes to his in defiance and placed both hands on her hips, fisting her skirts. *I'll not share yer bed. You can't force me. There's not enough wine in the castle to secure that fate.*

He reached gently for her shoulders and lowered his face against her chin. She exhaled and tensed; then relaxed, then tensed again not sure of what to expect or what she wanted at the moment. Her shoulders mimicked her breath and heaved up and down under the weight of his hands.

He grazed her neck with his chin stubble and trailed soft pecks towards her right ear placing his arms around her again.

Aye - you will.

Why would you say that?

Because ye want me lass - I ken the truth of it.

"*How do you know?*" she started to say.

She opened her mouth to speak audibly and realized she was massaging his tongue with her own in a rhythm that threatened to break her resolve. He leaned her against the stone wall once again and trapped her hands above her shoulders against the fortress. He relinquished control with his right hand and held them both now with his left hand while his right hand explored the length of her body.

Tall and lean with strong arms and bountiful breasts that sloped to her small waist then flared again at her hips. She was stunning and regal and noble and vulnerable all at the same time - and painfully stubborn. She would be the death of him, but he would seek it, want it, it would be his. Just to be with *her*.

Mine.

She mimicked shock and struggled to break free of him; but succeeded to only bring herself closer to him. She felt safe, protected and cherished in his arms, but wouldn't give him the satisfaction of knowing it. She closed her mind, tightly, as tightly as she could to avoid spilling her thoughts. She wouldn't give him the satisfaction.

"He'll have to work for this," she thought to herself.

"Of that, I've n-n-no d-doubt," he said audibly as he released his grasp of her while a wicked grin splayed across his tanned cheeks.

"Darina — we must go now," raised the sound of Minea's voice from behind her. A soft blush lit the old woman's face and she could not contain her grin. No doubt she had witnessed their exchange and it was obviously humorous to her.

"'Tis time my lady, we must ready you for the service."

THIRTY - THREE

O'Malley Lands

"He's finally awakened," said Vynae quietly to Lucian. "I believe he may be able to speak if ye wish to question him." The bald headed boy opened his eyelids and peeked around the room about him looking for something he recognized.

A sudden look of terror came over him when he realized he was tied to the bed and he began to scream. "Hold on, hold on," shouted Lucian as he quickly unwrapped the linens that held his arms to his sides.

"We tied ye to keep ye from scratching yer wrist, laddy," said Vynae. "We've had to stitch yer arm twice now; ye keep yanking them out with yer scratching. Be ye hungry?" she asked gently patting his head.

He nodded and turned to look at Lucian.

"Who are you?" asked Lucian.

"Who are you?" returned his answer.

"Where do you come from?" asked Lucian.

"Where am I?" returned the boy.

"Ye seem to have met ye match there, Lucian," Vynae chuckled. "What say I do the interrogations?" she smiled and handed the boy an oatcake dipped in plum sauce, then sat beside him on the bed stroking his hair.

"I am Vynae, the healer in this village. This is Lucian, he is our scribe and you are in the sick house on O'Malley lands. Clan O'Malley – do ye ken what I'm saying?"

He stared at her blankly.

She continued, "Ye were brought here by our new Laird and several of our men. Ye were found in the forest between O'Malley territory and Burke Territory."

His eyes grew wide with terror and he shot up out of the bed and had made it halfway to the door when Lucian caught him.

"Whoa there laddy, where do you think you are going?" he said blocking the door and standing with his arms crossed above his chest.

He began to cry and whimper uncontrollably and threw himself to the floor in a ball. Vynae gave Lucian a disapproving look and took the boy by the hand - leading him back to the bed.

"Ye are safe here," she said. "Willna hurt ye son. Tell us who ye are and where ye from and mayhap we can see ye home."

Lucian nodded his agreement with her and stood beside his bed.

"I am Jordy McClure," he ventured. Lucian nodded his understanding and request for him to continue. "My father is Judaen McClure, from the McTierney clan."

"MacTierney clan?" Lucian grasped. "How did you get all the way to Burke Lands?"

"My father is a textile merchant. We come to the port to trade often. The last time we were here for market, two men grabbed me and put me in a small boat with them. They put a cloak over my head and hit me; when I woke up - I was in the dungeons beneath the monastery.

* * *

"You asked for me," said Lucian to Patrick who was tying his hair off at the nape of his neck while examining his image in the looking glass brought up by Odhran.

I did. I've need to speak of Darina with you.

Silence.

"I know ye can hear me, druid," pressed Patrick.

"Well son? What need have ye of my services?" asked Lucian still standing in the doorway between the banquet room and the storage pantry which adjoined. His hands were clasped in front of him and twiddled the golden rope tied around his white cloak.

Ye don't hear me, or ye are pretending ye don't?

No response.

"I have a qu-que-question about Da-Darina," he spoke audibly.

"About Darina?" he replied.

"Aye. I d-do," said Patrick as he turned around to face the scribe. He walked slowly towards him and clasped forearms with Lucian, now adorned in his full priest attire. A gleam caught Patrick's eye and he looked down to see that Lucian wore the same shamrock crested ring as he did.

"Where did you get that?" asked Lucian hesitantly.

Get what?

No response came from Lucian.

"Well?" he asked again.

"My r-ring?" asked Patrick.

"Yes your ring Patrick. Where did you get that?" demanded Lucian.

"'Twas given to me by an old friend," he replied looking at the matching ring on Lucian's right hand. It was an intricate piece of artwork indeed. A signet ring of sterling silver with a dragon lain across the background of a shamrock. Two small rubies made the dragon's eye and fire thrust from his nostrils.

"Would this old friend have a name?" inquired Lucian further.

"Air-Airard - he is the blacksmith of my clan. The MacCahan clan," he clarified.

"You know Airard well, do you?" pried Lucian further.

"Aye, he is like me second father. He has trained me as a blacksmith for many years."

"What else has he trained ye for Patrick?" pressed Lucian, now standing only inches from Patrick.

Tell me.

Patrick's eyes shot up in astonishment and gripped Lucian's arms harder. They looked at each other for what seemed hours and then their arms dropped to their sides.

Patrick walked back towards the looking glass and straightened the MacCahan plaid about his shoulder and re-positioned the brooch holding it together.

Tell me son.

I think ye know verra well, Lucian. Airard is your brother, is he not?

Aye – he is. You must say it, my son.

Say what?

Ye know – say it.

Patrick grew uncomfortable with the questioning and fumbled with the ring on his hand, looking down and away from Lucian in what seemed like humiliation or fear – Lucian wasn't sure.

Ye are the last. Say it.

Nay - I'll not say it. I have no evidence ye are correct, Lucian.

You wear the ring Patrick. There are only three of the Dragon Crest rings - you know. I have one, Airard has one and you wear the other. I can only assume Airard conferred that to you.

"You are wr-wrong a-b-about that," spoke Patrick audibly.

"What do you mean?" asked Lucian confused. "You said it was a gift from an old friend."

"It belonged to m-m-my m-mo-mother," he replied and turned to sit upon the short three legged stool in front of Lucian. "'Twas given to me when she passed; my father insisted. Airard had it repaired and cleaned prior to giving it to me. Parkin was given her silver torc; and Payton was given her diadem. I was given my mother's hair comb and this" he said glancing at the ring on his right hand. "I am the only one who didn't receive a MacCahan clan crest."

Ye sound defeated lad. Mayhap ye mother knew ye wouldna always be a MacCahan.

Patrick locked eyes with him again. *How could she have known I'd take the O'Malley name?*

Yer mother wore that ring for a reason son. Do you ken?

What do you mean?

You know what the rings represent, do you not?

Aye - I think I do.

"Patrick, your mother was a druid priestess. Not just any priestess - mind you."

"How s-s-ss-so?" he asked standing up to face Lucian.

Your mother was one of only three. There are only three Dragonian's remaining Patrick; myself, my brathair and you. Patrick, ye are one of us.

And what are ye?

Patrick, I've no doubt Airard has prepared you. Don't pretend to misunderstand me. You know what I am saying.

"I've no such idea," he stated aloud, slowly and audibly. He hadn't stuttered and for that he was thankful.

"I s-sum-summoned you to speak of D-Darina," he stated sternly having twisted his ring wrong side with his left hand so that the crest faced his palm. "I've a question, and I w-wi-wish to k-kn-know the truth of it."

"Aye —Patrick; I will speak the truth. What do ye wish to know?

"I w-wi-wish to kn-know why she blames her-herself for her-her sister's d-death."

Ye've been using yer gift with the lass?

Patrick nodded affirmatively.

She won't like that. She's a bit skeptical.

Patrick nodded again and grinned.

"I see ye've spoken with her - in a manner of speaking," Lucian chuckled and straightened his robe. So you know of the boy's identity?" he asked.

Patrick nodded again.

Why doesn't she know? 'Tis nay fair to keep her in the dark of such things.

Tis what her da requested. We could only do what our Laird asked. Even his own wife went to her grave not knowing her youngest child remained alive and well in MacCahan castle.

'Tis nay right, Lucian. I mean to rectify it immediately. Why does she believe she is responsible for the death of this child who is very much alive?

Patrick rose and grasped arms with Lucian again, searching his face for the answer, demanding a response.

"Because before the child was born; Darina had fallen into the river and was being swept downstream. Anya went in after her and pulled her out. Saved her life she did."

"However?" asked Patrick.

"However, Anya took a fever from the cold water and was sick in bed for days. She went into early labor. The healer was terrified. We all were. We thought we had lost her."

"S-so ye l-let D'rina think it was her f-fault th-that the bairn died?"

"We had no other choice Patrick; we had to protect the child."

"Of course you had a choice. There is always a choice," he rebuked Lucian with his mind and stepped around him and into the banquet hall.

THIRTY - FOUR

O'Malley Castle - ***Six Nights Later***

It had been many moons since Darina ventured underground towards the clan council chamber. It was situated two floors under the castle proper; under the cold rooms, and between the dungeons and caves which led to the exterior of the keep near the shoreline.

Thankfully, they had never had need to, nor would her da permit the keeping of slaves or prisoners below. It was a barbaric practice which the elder O'Malley despised. Besides, her mother wouldn't have suffered it lightly. The doors to the cells had been removed and the dungeons had been used on a few occasions to shelter women and children during raids and for that the people were thankful.

Keeping pace with her as fast as his fat, furry feet could carry him was Fanai a copper eyed red and white spaniel that

Patrick had given her on their wedding night. A gift, he said, to compliment her hunting efforts with Riann.

An experienced falconry hound that hadn't quite won the affections of Riann yet; he was slowly growing on Darina. Although less than thrilled with the gift in the beginning; Fanai had proven himself a suitable companion and warm bed mate over the past days in Patrick's absence.

She slowed down her insistent march as she neared the chamber doors to find it blocked by two MacCahan soldiers. She held out a rolled parchment to the biggest one roughly and returned her fists to her hips.

"I wish to speak to the council," she stated abruptly, "now," she pointed at him.

The soldier on her right nodded his acknowledgement and motioned for her to sit on the bench next to the heavy wooden doors. He entered the chamber and returned shortly.

"The council is discussing important matters at the present and cannot be disturbed," he said to the air straight in front of him - never letting his eyes meet her.

"Tell them I will be heard now; I insist upon it."

"And what may I say do you wish to discuss with them?" he asked.

"The matter of my annulment," she responded stoically and bent to stroke Fanai who lay at her feet panting.

It had taken some time for her to come to her decision. She hadn't wanted to take it this far, but she saw no alternative. Six nights had passed since her wedding. Six nights has passed since he had left her. Alone, afraid and humiliated - a woman scorned.

"Six nights" *that was enough time*, she thought out loud.

"Bring her in," rang her uncle Ruarc's voice loud and clear through the chamber. The soldier motioned for her to rise and enter the chamber while the other sentry motioned for Fanai to stay put, not wanting the dog to follow her inside.

Fanai returned the sentiment by hiking his leg against the soldier and dousing his boots and truis. Darina cackled and spoke under her breath, "Well, ye might be of some use to me yet, Fanai." He followed her into the council chamber.

A large hearth stood at the back wall and a raging fire warmed the room. The triangular shaped council table sat in the middle of the room; two members seated on each of the three sides.

Guards watched the door and stood on each side of the hearth and servants carried trays of food and filled mugs with ale while the council members discussed clan business. Several parchments were laid across the table having been recently unrolled.

"What is this nonsense you speak of Darina?" Ruarc demanded angrily.

"'Tis not nonsense, dear uncle, and you ken what I am about."

Ruarc sat on one side of the table next to Gemma; Lucian sat next to Murchadh on the other side and Atilde sat in Rory's stead on the other - an empty chair to her right - the Laird's chair - or his wife's in his absence.

"I bring before the high council my petition for an annulment and I mean to make it happen," she responded sternly.

"On what grounds do ye bring this petition?" asked Gemma confused.

"On the grounds of abandonment, my lady," she sighed now looking at Gemma, "and I have proof enough. The MacCahan has been gone nigh to six eves and has not returned and has not sent word. I wish to dispose myself of this farce of a marriage. He left me on our wedding night and he hasn't returned." Tears welled up in eyes that were met with sympathy.

"Darina, to petition for abandonment, yer spouse must be gone more than two bliadains. Ye know this," said Atilde.

"Nay – there is another way," she retorted hanging her head in embarrassment. Lucian gave her an empathetic knowing glance and rose to speak. "I should like to address the council privately," he said. "Forthwith," he exclaimed raising his hands.

Ruarc acknowledged his request and sent the servants and soldiers out of the council room with a tilt of his head. Darina followed them to wait outside on the bench and the heavy wooden doors were barred from the inside once again.

She reclined on the wooden bench before realizing Fanai had not come out with her. The guards blocked her attempt to regain entry; all she could hope was that he wouldn't cause too much of a fuss. She sat alone on the bench, clenching her fists in her lap; hoping her memories wouldn't cause a flux of tears again.

Thiers's was a lovely ceremony. Lucian and Galen had seen to that; a mixture of old and new traditions that seemed to have pleased everyone. Her father would have been proud, her mother too. Her sisters were overjoyed and celebrated nearly the night long. The celebration of Samhain and the harvest coupled with their wedding had brought much peace and joy to the clan. The feasting had last nearly until sun up.

She and Patrick had run through the bonfires and danced and frolicked all night. He had indulged the children who had created a mask for him by wearing it most of the eve. Fittingly it was a red dragon and hers was a falcon.

Stop it. He tricked you.

He had forsworn the wine and even refused ale and mead at the reception. No doubt to prove a point with her, and he had insisted that she be served no more than two goblets of watered down elderberry wine.

A tussle against the chamber doors and raised voices indicated things were getting a might testy inside. The guard which stood on the right excused himself to make entry and the remaining guard raised his shoulders and tilted his head indicating he wasn't sure what was going on. She sat up straight and leaned her ear to the door to listen. All she could make out was the muffled sounds of loud argument.

Inside the chamber, things were becoming unruly. After hiding in the shadows; Payton resumed his seat next to Atilde, representing his brother the Laird who was not present. Patrick had named Payton his second in command during his absence and the council had no choice but to honor his request.

"Payton, what have you to say of your brother?" asked Ruarc staring angrily at him and visibly shaken.

"I don't get your meaning?" Payton replied confused.

Gemma spoke up, "Payton, the only alternative method for gaining an annulment for abandonment…" her words halted and she faltered for a moment before looking to Lucian to continue.

Payton sat forward in his chair laying his arms across the table and stared directly at Lucian who didn't speak.

"Well, Lucian, is somebody going to tell me what is going on here?" he asked.

Lucian grunted and pulled at his beard. He grunted at Gemma and spoke. "Payton there are only two ways to obtain an annulment by abandonment."

"And?" asked Payton.

"And the first is for the spouse to be missing more than two bliadains; with no word or missives about their whereabouts, safety, life or death. This is essential in times of war and travel, life and our clan must go on."

Payton leaned back in his chair, nodded in response and made a circular motion with his right hand in the air for him to continue.

"If one is missing two years Payton, with no word, they are presumed dead or having had abandoned their clan. They are pronounced banished and their spouse is released from the bonds of the marriage," interjected Gemma.

"I ken," said Payton. "But what has this to do with my brother?"

"There is another way," said Ruarc slightly embarrassed.

"And what is that?" he retorted impatiently.

Atilde interrupted and laid her hand on Payton's forearm,

"If the marriage is not consummated in ten night's time, the bond can be annulled by petition of either party on the grounds of abandonment."

Payton choked and leaned forward in his chair. Ruarc rose to pace the chamber and Atilde grew red with embarrassment.

"What have you to say of your brother, Payton?" Ruarc asked angrily pointing a worn right index finger at him.

"What have I got to say about this?" he asked sarcastically. "I have nothing to say about this."

"Did you know that Patrick was im-im-imp…oh by the gods unable to perform the duties of a husband?" questioned Murchadh under his breath toying with his goblet.

"Patrick has no such issues to my knowledge and I don't believe her," he shouted and stood pointing an arm right back at Ruarc. "I invoke my right to question her in my brother's stead."

The council members gasped and chaos stole order from the room. Murchadh was pounding his fist on the table and Ruarc's face had turned three shades of purple from holding his breath - his temper threatening to get the better of him.

"Silence!" commanded Lucian. "I've heard enough. Payton, 'tis your right to question the lass. I would caution ye to be noble and honorable. She is the next in command of the O'Malley clan and should this marriage be annulled, 'twould cost the MacCahan's a great deal; especially your brother."

Payton nodded his acknowledgement and gestured for the sentry to send her back in.

Fanai met Darina at the door and lapped at her ankles sending waves of calm throughout her body. Her shoulders relaxed and she took a deep breath before entering the chambers again.

Here it comes.

Lucian motioned for her to take his seat next to Murchadh and it was then she noticed Payton sitting aside her aunt Atilde.

"What is he doing here?" she asked pointing an accusing finger at Payton.

"Darina, Patrick placed him as second in command before he left. He has invoked his right to question you concerning your petition for annulment and the council has agreed to let him do so."

She nodded at Payton, casting a warning glance his way and said, "Then by all means let's get this over with," and sighed heavily melting into her chair.

"Darina, I'll not waste any time with pleasantries. I'll ask you but one question," said Payton.

"Alright then, please do so."

"Darina, was my brother Patrick unable or was he unwilling to consummate the marriage on your wedding night?"

Gemma stood straight up and pushed her chair back with her legs in one loud swift movement. Her hands landed on the table in front of her with a garish thud and she groaned audibly.

"This is unnecessary," she bellowed and turned to walk towards the hearth.

"Nay, he is being as courteous as he can, considering the matter" said Lucian rubbing Darina's shoulders in comfort.

Darina was unable to contain the flood of tears that were walled up behind her lashes. They spilled forth as if a dam had broken and drenched her face. Ruarc handed her a cloth which she used to wipe her face and blow her nose. Every attempt she made to speak was met with another wave of tears that made communication nearly impossible.

"Oh! What difference does it make Payton," demanded Atilde angry at this point. "Can't you see she speaks the truth? She has been dishonored and no man will want her now."

Payton replied, "It makes a great bit of difference here. Ten nights have not passed, only six. There are four more nights that the marriage can still be consummated. My brother may return any moment now and here we all sit contemplating the annulment of this marriage. Her petition is four days premature and I intend to find out why."

He stared at Darina who continued to weep quietly.

"I'll give you each notice right now that before this day is over I intend to tell Darina everything she needs to know.

This annulment will not happen and you all know why! You have hidden a delicate matter from her and as the Laird's wife she has a right to be informed."

Darina raised her eyes to meet Payton's. She saw the same fire and ice in him as she had in Patrick. He was coming to *her* defense. *But; whatever for?*

"Darina - wait outside!" commanded Lucian. "We will call you back in just a moment; we've some things to discuss with your husband's brother."

Once again, Darina took up residence on the bench outside the council chamber. This time, Fanai sat beside her with his head in her lap. The tears continued, but her heart had turned, there was promise of some answers - finally. Mayhap now she will know what took him from her so abruptly in the middle of the night. *Why he had abandoned her.*

Memories flooded her vision again; the ceremony, the reception, Samhain, the bon fires, the masks, the children asking for pastries. Good memories; all of which ended too soon, so shockingly cut short was their time together. *He left me.*

They had danced and he had held her; closely with such tenderness. Just the feel of his hand in hers brought the heat to her face. He had whispered promises in her ear all night long; between the festivities - catching her as often as he could to steal a kiss. He had carried her to their chamber; a smile as wide as the sea upon his face with her feigning mock abduction and kicking and screaming in jest.

When the chamber doors had opened and he sat her down, she was aghast to find a spaniel pup in the middle of the large bed chewing on the white rose petals Patrick had bid lain there. A big beautiful clumsy pup that slobbered her arms when she petted him. It was the most thoughtful, horrible gift she had ever received; but it pleased Patrick so to see her smile she couldn't bear to disappoint her new husband.

A cloud of steam rose from behind the screen wall in the corner encasing the large new bathing tub Patrick had brought up. The smell of lavender and rose petals mixed with the warm air and he gestured for her to undress and relax. Her maidservant entered and assisted her undressing and entry into the frothy waters then quickly excused herself.

She could hear the sound of wine being poured into goblets and the fire being stoked. The lavender had sent her into an almost spell bound state of relaxation and she laid her head back upon the end of the tub and closed her eyes. Her feet did not reach the other side. *This is the biggest tub I've ever seen.*

She could still hear the harpist playing below and the bellow of the pipe's coming off of the islands. *Everything was so lovely,* she thought. *Stop it. It means nothing. He left you. He is a coward and he left you.*

Memory overtook reality again and she recalled the large hands that encircled her head from behind and which carefully removed the pins that supported the weight of her hair.

He used his fingers to gently separate the locks that had been intertwined in an elaborate braid. Still behind her; he handed her a goblet of wine overhead and motioned for her to move forward in the tub to let him in behind her.

He is stark naked. By the gods, he intends to bathe with me!

Aye — I do. I intend to finish that bath we started an eve ago, he sighed with pleasure.

She blushed; let out a small giggle and set herself back down in the tub after he had positioned himself. Leaning against his chest, she could feel his heartbeat behind her.

"Darina, did he make any attempt at all to consummate your union?"

"Darina?"

294

She was back in the chamber and being questioned. Someone had interrupted her memories, her train of thought. *What did she ask?*

"Darina," continued Gemma. "Did Patrick make any attempt whatsoever to consummate your union? I know this is difficult but we must have the answers," she said apologetically.

Payton interrupted, "Darina, I will ask you again. Was my brother unable or unwilling to consummate the marriage?"

She bowed her head in thought and answered sheepishly, "Well - he was not - unable, if that is what you wish to know. He was mostly - *unwilling* - I would say."

"Unwilling!" hollered Ruarc over the sounds of the council. "Unwilling! A dishonor I tell you, he has brought grave dishonor to this clan!"

"Hold on a minute," interrupted Lucian.

Darina had begun to cry uncontrollably again and Payton's face became white as snow. "I don't believe it!" he shouted back to Ruarc. "I don't believe it," he repeated. "Tell us exactly what happened," he demanded to Darina who had now grown angry as well as humiliated.

She rose in defiance to pace the room, both fists on her hips and strode towards Payton instead. She held out an accusing finger and retaliated. "Nobody calls me a liar, you imbecile!"

"Then tell me the truth!" he shouted back to her face.

That did it.

Ruarc lurched towards them, but not in time to prevent Darina from landing a solid punch to the left of Payton's jaw that sent him reeling backwards to the floor. Payton cringed in pain and held the side of his face.

"What sort of ladies are ye raising here, Ruarc?" Payton asked sarcastically.

"The kind that knows how to defend themselves; and their honor Payton," he replied.

Lucian grabbed Darina by the shoulders and led her back to her seat. He motioned for a servant who brought a large goblet of wine and set it before her. She quickly returned with a flask of whiskey as well and set it before her.

She grabbed the whiskey.

"Darina, I realize this subject matter much cause you great embarrassment," said her Aunt Atilde.

"And what of my brother?" interjected Payton impatiently. "We speak of matters he is in no way able to address not being here."

"You," she said pointing at Payton who was holding up the stone wall still grasping the side of his mouth, "will hold your tongue and stay right there."

"You," she said pointing at Darina who had just downed the last of the whiskey, "Will think long and hard and speak carefully - for you tread on thin ice," she warned.

Darina closed her eyes and let the rest of the burn settle into her stomach. The whiskey would help her. She could speak her mind without faltering. *This wouldn't be so bad.*

The warmth of the water surrounded her again. Soothing and relaxing, the lavender scent traveled to her nose and released tension in ways she didn't understand. He was washing her hair now, tenderly lathering the soapy oils into the length of her curly red mane and kneading his fingers delicately on her scalp. *Heaven. This must be heaven.*

When he had finally finished rinsing her hair; he twisted into a loop and hung it over her left shoulder. She edged closer to him, using her hands on his thighs to push back against him.

Her feet still did not touch the other end of the tub and he enveloped her with his arms to keep her from sliding away.

He sighed a contented, satisfied breath and whispered in her ear? "Do y-you l-like the tub, luv?" he asked. She nodded her approval and twisted her head to the left exposing her neck to him.

An invitation, I see.

"Aye," she responded with her mind, knowing full well he was trespassing again.

He laid kisses gingerly about her neck and traveled up with his mouth to behind her ear to accost it with his tongue. She whimpered in delight and lightening shot from her breasts to her heat. She arched her back in reflex and let a moan escape her lips. He caught it with his mouth and plundered her tongue with his own.

Aye - Braeden was right, ye may be a wee bit of a hell cat.

"I heard that," she said audibly toying with him.

"I know," he said slowly and clearly in return.

She arched against him frantically and he responded in kind. His left hand drew circles across her perky cold nipple and the other glided up her thigh to her hip where it settled for a spell. She returned his kiss again, searching for more and grinded against his hips when his right hand found her mound.

He bit her neck and she let out a shrill groan backing into him with fervor. Both arms circled her now; his left wrapped between her breasts crossing over to her right shoulder and his right still rested on her hip while his hand massaged her heat below the waters.

Her breath was staggered now, coming and going in waves. She backed into his arousal again and confirmed his intentions; moving her hips in an up and down motion that sent him into fits of anguish.

Two can play this game.

His attention to her swollen cleft intensified and she wriggled in pleasure increasing the pressure her backside placed on his throbbing cock. He dipped his hand lower to find her slippery and slick, ready for him and he eased one finger, knuckle deep, into her heat. She buckled against him and increased her tempo, rising and lowering herself against his hold and firmly pressing her backside against his tortured erection.

Their lips met again in a frenzy of lust and want and he slipped another finger inside her velvet softness until swollen flesh met his hand. She groaned and rose up against him and he strengthened his hold on her with his left hand; grasping her nipple and twisting it playfully.

If you dinnae stop soon, I will waste my seed in the water my sweets. I've no wish to dishonor you thus.

She ignored him and continued her motions against him, groaning and whimpering. He felt her warmth clench around his fingers and he rubbed her nub with his thumb rhythmically.

Darina, tell me what you want.

She groaned and continued her assault on his engorged cock. She felt his balls tighten and knew his release was nigh. She tightened her clasp on his fingers and began rocking back and forth against them.

"D-Darina, please," he begged in a whisper. *What do you want?*

She mumbled something incoherent under her breath and tightened her legs in front of her. He grasped her nipple tightly to get her attention.

"Patrick," she moaned lustfully.

"Yes?" he begged, unable to endure the sweet torture any longer.

"Patrick, we have al-al-all night……" she gasped still grinding against his cock.

Yes. But I don't right now.

'Twould mean me no dishonor my lord.

What? He moaned himself this time - a deep guttural moan that sent ripples through the top of the water.

It would be no offense Patrick, if you would… Oh. She moaned and leaned into his mouth for a kiss, still grinding and clenching herself around his fingers.

If you would peak with me, my lord - twould be glorious Patrick. Please, don't make me stop, she begged him with her mind.

"Darina!" Patrick moaned in her ear.

"Bathe me Patrick. Bathe me in your seed," she groaned into his mouth and intensified her pressure on his cock. He writhed and shook and felt her spasm against his fingers as his own release swept over him and into the water around them.

She collapsed against his chest and lay lifeless there for long moments. His breath finally stabilized and he released his hold on her womanhood. She jerked about as continuing waves of ecstasy pulsed through her blood and she settled deeper into his embrace. She couldn't get close enough to him.

"Darina, answer the question." Her thoughts snapped back to present time.

"Darina," said Atilde. "Are you alright dear?" she asked wiping the tears from Darina's face. "Can you answer his question?"

"Darina, was it his choice not to consummate the marriage?" asked Payton again, slowly and methodically this time.

"I - I don't know - how to answer that."

"Does the blame belong with you or with him?" asked Ruarc abruptly tired of the questioning.

Darina untied and retied the belt covering her tunic and truis and petted Fanai who lay at the ground beside her. "I would have to say, that the blame lies with you, Uncle Ruarc," she answered stoically looking him right in the face.

Payton coughed and Ruarc rose from his chair to address her directly. "How on earth would the consummation of your marriage in any way be my responsibility lass?" he asked angrily.

"You took him Uncle. You took him from our chambers and he has never returned."

A hush rose over the chambers and Lucian shook his head back and forth; an apparent fear rising in him.

THIRTY - FIVE

Council Chambers - O'Malley Castle

Pain and anguish adorned Ruarc's face and he sat to collect his thoughts. His niece's accusation met him with force. *She was right. I did take him from her on their wedding night. I had no other choice. He had to know.*

Payton interrupted, "That's it - I've had enough of this charade. It's time she knew and since none of ye other pussy willows have the bollocks to tell her - I will!"

He strode towards Darina and bent to kneel down beside her. Fanai got up and moved to her other side, sensing it was needed. "Promise ye won't punch me again my lady?" he asked sheepishly grinning up at her.

"Don't Payton, let me," said Lucian.

"Nay — I won't. Ye've had eleven years to get to the right of it, and I'll not give you the opportunity now."

Darina shook her head in confusion and looked up at Payton. "Payton will tell me. I trust him."

"Good," he said as he rose and walked towards the stony wall. "Darina, Ruarc came to get Patrick that night in your chamber, did he not?"

"Aye, he did. We were um, in the bath, I mean I was in the bath and we were wet and a fierce banging came on the chamber door and Patrick rose to open it," she said from behind flushed cheeks.

"He did and who was there, Darina?"

"From behind the privacy screen — I could hear Uncle Ruarc and Patrick discussing something that seemed to be of importance."

"And then what happened?" he asked as he waived his hands across his chest animatedly as if making a point to the council.

"Then Patrick returned to the room, shut the door, adorned himself with his chain and armor and told me that he was needed to retrieve something and he would be right back."

"And you haven't seen or heard from him since?"

"Nay — I haven't. Payton — what is going on?"

"Ruarc, would you please tell Darina why Patrick left at your request."

Ruarc flinched at the mention of his name and his face grew red with shame. "We were told by Mavis that the boy, Braeden had been abducted at the piers and taken off in a boat the morn of Samhain. Mavis managed to escape by leaping from the vessel and swam for hours until she reached the shores, just past midnight."

"And?" bade Payton motioning for him to continue.

"And I sent for Rory and Kyra to accompany Patrick to retrieve the boy."

"You sent him?" asked Darina not believing it. "You *sent* my husband after his bastard child on my wedding night on the advice of his mistress?" Tears threatened to spill themselves down her cheeks again.

Payton interrupted and spoke directly to Darina this time, "Braeden is not Patrick's bastard child and Mavis is not his mistress."

"I've heard tell of your brother and his many illegitimate bairns. His reputation precedes him unfortunately," retorted Darina angrily.

Payton's voice rose in anger. "You don't know what you are talking about you snotty wench," he said behind clenched teeth.

Fanai rose from the cold stone floor beside Darina and growled loudly and deliberately, clearly showing Payton his teeth. He scampered until he had put himself between Payton and Darina and sat, teeth raised, inviting him to continue.

"Payton, you would do well to lower your voice," Darina mused. "Explain yourself."

"I've no doubt you have heard tell of my brother, Darina. And - he does have a reputation as that of a lady's man, a lecher some might say."

"See," Darina responded nodding her head and gesturing to the council members.

"But that brother, Darina, would be Parkin; not Patrick. Parkin is the one with illegitimate children and a handful of heart-broken women following him about. Patrick is the most honorable man I have ever known. Patrick is more honorable than me own da even - though it would shame him to hear it."

"Then why by the goddess, would he leave his wife on their wedding night to chase after a no account bastard child?" she spat at him, the indignation rising in her voice.

"Shall I tell her then?" asked Payton to Lucian who stood stone-faced and pale against the hearth. Lucian nodded.

"Because Darina, that no account bastard child is your brother."

* * *

It had only taken moments for Darina to return to her chamber and don her armor and cloak. She called for Riann to be readied and for Moya to prepare her steed. She was situating her helmet when Payton burst through the door.

"Where do you think you are going?" Payton asked accusingly. She ignored him and jumped into her boots as she tied Fanai to the bed post and instructed Minea to care for him in her absence.

"I asked you a question, *sister*," he jabbed sarcastically at her.

"I'd like to know the same thing," interrupted Ruarc who was out of breath after having followed her up nearly seven flights of stairs.

"I am the best hunter in the clan and no one else has my tracking abilities," she said as she gestured towards the window where Riann was seen circling the keep. "I intend to bring my brother and my *husband* home."

"I will deal with you later," she pointed at Ruarc. "Ye've sent yer brother, a ship builder, with Kyra and my husband, who does not know our lands to retrieve the true Laird of O'Malley clan."

"And you, I would thrash you within an inch of yer life if ye hadn't been the only man brave enough to tell me the truth," she directed at Payton.

"Well?" she gestured towards Payton impatiently. "Aren't ye coming with me? He is yer brother, an honorable mon ye say? Don your amour and ride with me," she insisted.

"Nay," said Ruarc from the other side of the bed. "Patrick has left him in charge in his stead."

"And I am leaving you in charge in my stead. I trust you won't muck this up?" she shouted angrily, loud enough for the rafter to shake.

Ruarc nodded and Darina and Payton headed off into the night to save her brother and her husband from the Burke witch.

MORE TITLES

BY DELANEY RHODES

Celtic Steel Series

Book 2: Celtic Shores

Book 3: Celtic Skies

Book 4: Celtic Stars

Book 5: Celtic Sun

Celtic Shores
Celtic Steel, Book 2

Patrick MacCahan just became the new Laird of the O'Malley clan. His new position is met with many obstacles including a tempestuous new wife, a two decade long war with a neighboring village, a missing foster child and a pagan witch who overpowers the clan at every turn.

Parkin MacCahan's life just got a lot more exciting. His older brother Patrick has married the eldest daughter of the O'Malley clan. And his father Laird MacCahan is building a shipping empire off the coast of Northern Ireland. Parkin must oversee the operations and coordinate efforts between the O'Malleys and the MacCahans.

In order to dock at O'Malley port, Parkin and his men must sail passed the legendary Island of Women. Will Parkin be able to withstand the temptation to trespass the legendary shore? Or will he be invited?

Kyra O'Connell has resided in O'Malley territory all of her life. As the niece of the late Laird Dallin O'Malley, and daughter of the clan's chieftan; she has been part of the inner circle since before she can remember. When a spy is found among the villagers, Kyra is asked to take up residence on the Island of Women and to infiltrate their ranks as a spy herself.

ABOUT THE AUTHOR

Of Irish and English descent, Romance Author Delaney Rhodes is a native Texan from birth. She is a Graduate with double Majors from The University of Houston, in Law and Writing. She has two teenage daughters, and is married to an entrepreneurial Husband. Three of her favorite people, are her three rescued Russian Blue cats; Sebastian, Sasha, and Sissy. The family would not be complete without "13", an adopted Bearded Dragon.

Together they live life at a fast pace, enjoying each other and striving to help the world become a better place. Besides her writing and family – Ms. Rhodes is active in many charitable organizations that benefit animals and children, both through volunteering and fundraising.

Ms. Rhodes' writing was prompted and inspired by many hours of research and study into her Irish and Celtic family lineage and heritage. Many of the stories you will find in the chapters of her writings were birthed while striving to connect with those that had walked these paths and lived before her.

Celtic Storms

Copyright © 2012 by Delaney Rhodes

DR Publishing

ISBN: 978-0-615-59798-0

Cover Design by Kim Killion

Edited by A. McConnell

17605336R00167